Harvey
Takes
the *Lead*

Praise for *Harvey Comes Home*

"[T]his gently paced, character-driven narrative captivates on every level, transforming a 'lost dog' story into a deeper reading experience."—*School Library Journal* ★ *Starred Review*

"Dog lovers will drool over this multi-generational story."—*Booklist*

"Affecting, riveting, and evocative, this character-driven tale within a tale… believably reveals the best and sometimes the worst of human nature….Much more than a lost-dog story."—*Kirkus Reviews*

Praise for *Harvey Holds His Own*

"With the winning combination of a relatable main character and an adorable dog, this book should find a home with readers seeking a warmhearted tale of growth and connection."—*School Library Journal*

"Characters…are lovingly developed, resulting in a deeply engaging coming-of-age story."—*Kirkus Reviews*

"Heartwarming…*Harvey Holds His Own* is a charming novel whose important life lessons are bettered by the love of a good dog."—*Foreword Reviews*

Harvey
Takes
the *Lead*

by **COLLEEN NELSON**
Illustrations by Tara Anderson

First published in Canada and the United States in 2022

www.pajamapress.ca   info@pajamapress.ca

The publisher gratefully acknowledges the support of the Canada Council for the Arts and the Ontario Arts Council for its publishing program. We acknowledge the financial support of the Government of Canada through the Canada Book Fund (CBF) for our publishing activities.

Library and Archives Canada Cataloguing in Publication
Title: Harvey takes the lead / by Colleen Nelson ; illustrations by Tara Anderson.
Names: Nelson, Colleen, author. | Anderson, Tara, illustrator.
Description: First edition.
Identifiers: Canadiana 20210393599 | ISBN 9781772782400 (hardcover)
Classification: LCC PS8627.E555 H37 2022 | DDC jC813/.6—dc23

Publisher Cataloging-in-Publication Data (U.S.)
Names: Nelson, Colleen, author. | Anderson, Tara, illustrator.
Title: Harvey Takes the Lead / by Colleen Nelson ; illustrations by Tara Anderson.
Description: Toronto, Ontario Canada : Pajama Press, 2022. | Summary: Strict new rules at Brayside Retirement Home make it hard for West Highland Terrier Harvey to continue his important role as comfort dog. Meanwhile, Harvey's owner Maggie struggles with being the understudy for the school play, his friend Austin faces shame over money troubles, and retirement home resident Bob Kowalski begins to feel lonely and anxious as his wife is in the hospital"— Provided by publisher.
Identifiers: ISBN 978-1-77278-240-0 (hardcover)
Subjects: LCSH: West Highland terrier – Juvenile fiction. | Retirement communities -- Juvenile fiction. | Helping behavior – Juvenile fiction. | Anxiety – Juvenile fiction. | BISAC: JUVENILE FICTION / Social Themes / Friendship. | JUVENILE FICTION / Social Themes / Self-Esteem & Self-Reliance. | JUVENILE FICTION / School & Education.
Classification: LCC PZ7.N457Ha |DDC [F] – dc23

Original art created with graphite pencil on Canson drawing paper
Cover and book design—Lorena González Guillén

Manufactured by Friesens
Printed in Canada

Pajama Press Inc.
11 Davies Avenue, Suite 103 Toronto, Ontario Canada, M4M 2A9

Distributed in Canada by UTP Distribution
5201 Dufferin Street Toronto, Ontario Canada, M3H 5T8

Distributed in the U.S. by Ingram Publisher Services
1 Ingram Blvd. La Vergne, TN 37086, USA

MIX
Paper from responsible sources
FSC® C016245
www.fsc.org

For *Wayne Pickering*,
the keeper of our family stories

–C.N.

For *Mr. Z* (Robert Zawerbny),
the best illustration teacher ever! I still listen to
your advice and encouragement in my mind

–T.A.

Chapter 1

Harvey

H arvey scampers outside with Maggie close behind. Tail held high and ears pricked, Harvey is on patrol for anything amiss. A new layer of snow has fallen overnight. The flakes are large and powdery and make the ground slippery underneath his paws. He shakes his body, fluffing up his coat and trots to the end of the driveway. A few squirts, and one patch of snow isn't so white anymore.

Harvey is a West Highland Terrier, a ratter by nature—smart, easily trained, and willing to do anything to protect his Maggie. Just ask the raccoon who found out the hard way last fall.

Harvey leads Maggie to the end of the street. In warmer weather, they'd walk farther, but on a cold January morning like this one, just getting to the corner is an accomplishment—for Maggie anyway. Harvey isn't bothered by the cold. He dives nose-first into the snow and snuffles through like a mini snowblower until he reaches a fire hydrant. It's full of scents from other dogs. Rosie, the Westie who lives down the street, and Romeo, an older dog who moved into the neighborhood not too long ago. Gordie, the golden lab, has been especially generous. Harvey could spend a while sniffing, but Maggie's not in the mood for it. "Come on, Harvey," she says. "Dad's taking us to Brayside."

Like *walk*, *treat*, and *squirrel*, *Brayside* is a word Harvey knows well. Brayside Retirement Villa is like a second home to Harvey. It's where he first met Austin, the boy who kept him safe until his Maggie could find him.

Harvey picks up the pace. A car is idling in the driveway. Maggie opens the door and gives Harvey a boost into the backseat. Once he's safely buckled, Maggie gets in the front, and they set off.

There's nothing for Harvey to do but lie down and put his head on his paws. Going to Brayside means another adventure with his Maggie. And who knows where that could lead?

Chapter 2

Maggie

When they arrive at Brayside, Maggie opens the car door, and Harvey leaps out. He doesn't wait for Maggie, not with Austin on the other side of the sliding doors. Austin can barely spit out a hello to Maggie; he's too busy getting a tongue bath of doggie kisses from Harvey.

Seventh grade has been all about changes for Maggie: a new school and new friends. She's glad she has Austin. Even though they had a rough start, he's proven to be a good friend. And it's also a relief to have a place like Brayside to visit. The residents always make Maggie (and Harvey) feel welcome. With the wingback chairs, fireplace, and grand piano, the entrance of Brayside reminds Maggie of a luxury hotel. "Is Bertie here?" she asks.

Austin stands up and shakes his head. "I'll bring her tomorrow." As cute as his puppy is, she's still learning the rules at Brayside. No jumping up on the residents. No running out the front doors. No chewing on chair legs. No stealing slippers. Mr. Kowalski has gone through a couple of pairs thanks to Bertie's sharp puppy teeth.

They are interrupted by a *toot-toot*. Mr. Singh appears on his Cobra GT4 motorized scooter. Its electric engine is dangerously quiet. The horn isn't. "Good day, Maggie! Can't stop to chat." He heads to the games room. "Late for afternoon poker!"

"Harvey!" Mary Rose calls as she comes out of Mrs. Gelman's room. She's pushing her nursing cart, but shoves it out of the way to pat Harvey. His tail rotates like an out-of-control helicopter propeller.

"Well, today's the big day," Mary Rose says to Maggie and Austin. "Charlie's announcing the new assistant director of Brayside." Maggie admires the way someone as short as Mary Rose commands such a presence. Since Charlie has been running both Brayside and Walker Terraces, the new retirement complex, a lot of his work has fallen on Mary Rose's shoulders.

There've been a lot of other changes recently too. Austin's grandpa, Phillip, was promoted to head custodian at Walker Terraces, and Isaac was hired as his replacement at Brayside. Isaac is younger and doesn't have Phillip's experience, but as Mary Rose likes to say, he's a hard worker and his heart is in the right place.

"Do you know who it is?" Austin asks.

"I know who I hope it isn't," Mary Rose says with a meaningful look. "Brayside might be a retirement home, but it isn't a jail."

"What do you mean?"

Mary Rose purses her lips and puts a hand on her hip. "One of the people Charlie interviewed kept going on about how safety should be the number one concern. She said that running a tight ship is better for everyone, including the residents."

"A tight ship?" Austin repeats.

"Oh, don't worry, I told Charlie what I thought about that one." It's hard to argue with Mary Rose. She turns to the front doors. "Well, look who's here."

Charlie is wearing a bulky winter coat, which makes him look rounder than he is. A woman is with him. With her blunt bangs and poker-straight brown hair, she looks no-nonsense.

"Oh no," Mary Rose groans. "That's her! The Warden!"

As Charlie and the woman enter Brayside, Maggie gets a sinking feeling. The so-called warden looks around the foyer

like there's a bad smell to it. She takes in the grand piano
that Mrs. Gustafson plays for pre-dinner concerts and the
fire blazing in the fireplace—something the residents love to
see in the winter. Her eyes widen slightly when they land on
Harvey. And not in a good way.

Chapter 3

Austin

One thing about Harvey, he's never met a stranger. Everyone is a long-lost friend that he needs to greet. But not everyone wants to be greeted. This lady sure doesn't. She looks at Harvey like he's a filthy bathmat.

Charlie grins at us like he's won the lottery. "Mary Rose, I'd like you to meet Hilary Appleby, Brayside's new assistant director." Mary Rose holds out her hand to shake and when Ms. Appleby does the same, something jingles. A bracelet, covered in charms. One is an apple, in honor of her name, I guess.

"Congratulations," Mary Rose says, but she doesn't sound happy. Ms. Appleby's eyes go to Maggie, me, and Harvey.

"These are some volunteers. And Harvey's our comfort dog."

"Comfort dog," she repeats, suspiciously.

Maggie stiffens beside me. "Harvey and I come on the weekends to visit. Everyone loves him."

"Is he a *certified* comfort dog?"

Maggie pauses. Harvey is so good at his job, who cares if he doesn't have a paper to prove it? Part of me wants her to lie and say yes, but Maggie is too honest for that. "Uh, no," she says.

Ms. Appleby purses her lips. "I see."

Charlie gives Mary Rose a look that says "Isn't she great?" But Charlie spends most of his time in the office. He doesn't see all the hard work that the nursing staff, led by Mary Rose, Louise, and Artie do to keep the residents happy. Or that the residents get lonely sometimes. Visits from Harvey, and even Bertie, give them something to look forward to.

"We'd better get started," Charlie says. "There's lots to go over if you're going to start on Monday."

The three of us stay quiet as they walk away. Mary Rose makes a disapproving noise in her throat once they're out of earshot.

"Margaret! There you are!" Mrs. Fradette, the most eccentric of the old people at Brayside, comes bustling out of the library. Mrs. Fradette is in her eighties, but she moves as if she's younger. She's got tons of energy, which matches her brightly colored outfits. Harvey sits at her feet waiting for a head scratch.

She looks at us through her thick-framed glasses. "What's got you three so glum?"

"We met Charlie's replacement," I say.

Mary Rose makes that noise in her throat again.

"I don't think she likes Harvey," Maggie says.

"Bah!" Mrs. Fradette's laugh sounds like an explosion. "Not possible!" Mrs. Fradette was more of a cat person until she met Harvey. He won her over pretty quickly, but I'm not sure it'll be the same with Ms. Appleby.

"What if she says Harvey can't visit anymore?" Maggie asks.

Mrs. Fradette waves a hand, dismissing the idea. "If Charlie didn't have a problem with it, I don't see why she would."

"You didn't see the look on her face," I say, shaking my head.

"You would've thought Harvey was a hundred-pound pit bull," Maggie adds.

"Wait till she meets Hurricane Bertie," I groan. Maggie keeps reassuring me that Bertie's behavior will improve as she gets older. I hope she's right. I had big dreams about Bertie visiting the residents like Harvey does, but the truth is, for a little dog, Bertie is a lot of work. Way more than I was expecting.

I'm not complaining! I wouldn't trade her for anything. She might be a handful, but she's my handful.

Chapter 4

Harvey

Harvey has had a busy day at Brayside and is currently quite comfortable lying at Austin's feet in the carpeted foyer, as the fire warms his backside.

"Time to go, Harvey." At the sound of Maggie's voice, he stands up, stretching his front legs, then his hind end. It's quite a production and can't be rushed. Austin stands up too, but it's Maggie that Harvey focuses on.

Her hair is long and loose and fills the air with the scent of shampoo. The coppery hue of it has deepened over the winter. It's now a striking auburn that gets a lot of envious stares from girls at St. Ambrose Academy.

"Come on, Harvey. Dad's outside."

Harvey has spent the afternoon visiting with the old people, in the games room first, and then making the rounds with Austin to a few of the suites. Everywhere he goes, Harvey is greeted with love and affection.

His coat got a little snowy in the outdoor courtyard, but it wasn't anything a race around the games room couldn't fix. The residents cheered him on as he zipped between furniture, finally coming to rest on the couch beside Mrs. O'Brien.

Best of all, he's been able to untangle and catalog the many scents at Brayside.

While Maggie uses her eyes to identify people, Harvey uses his nose. Once a scent has made its way into his brain, it is there forever.

He knows Mr. Singh by his rubber tires, Mrs. O'Brien by her baking, and Mrs. Fradette because of the strong perfume that tickles his nose. He'd know Austin anywhere even if he didn't carry Bertie's scent. The new woman, Ms. Appleby, has left her smell behind—it is crisp and bright like a cold winter's day. All these odors make up Brayside to Harvey. They are pieces of a puzzle that fit together in his mind to form a place—or an idea of place—where he finds comfort.

But as he wakes up and shakes the sleep out of himself, he detects another faint smell coming from along the baseboard. He'd like to sniff and ferret it out, but Maggie has clipped his leash to his collar. Harvey follows Maggie and Austin to the front doors. The investigation will have to wait until next time.

Chapter 5

Austin

As soon as I step into my apartment, Bertie races to me, her little legs spinning too fast for her body. The hardwood floors of our apartment are like a skating rink, and she's going nowhere fast. Mom comes out of the kitchen. "She's been nipping my feet for the last ten minutes. Play with her!"

Bertie jumps up, licking my face and neck. Her little tongue even goes up my nose. "Bertie! Are you happy to see me?" I laugh. The answer is obvious because her is tail is in overdrive. I lie on the floor and she climbs on top of me, pinning me down so she can give me my second full-face tongue wash.

I reach for a stuffy and dangle it out to her. She lunges, and when I throw it, she runs, sliding into the couch. "She probably needs a *W-A-L-K* too," Mom calls.

I grab the leash off the hook at the door. As soon as she hears the jangle, she comes scampering over and looks up at me with her big, brown eyes. I melt a little. She's got a brown spot over each eye, and her ears are way too big for her head. The rest of her is white with another big patch of brown on her back. "Do you want to go for a walk?" I ask. It's a dumb question because she *always* wants to go for a walk!

Bertie yips and spins in circles. I can barely attach the leash. As soon as I open the door, she takes off like someone fired a starting pistol.

Outside she sniffs, trying to find the right spot to do her business. I don't know why it matters so much—I'm just going to pick it up when she's done. She finally decides on the perfect location in front of the sidewalk.

We're heading back inside when I see Grandpa coming up the sidewalk. Bertie tries to leap over the snowbank to get to him, but her legs are too short. She does a face-plant instead.

"What's new with my favorite grandson?" he asks.

"I'm you're only grandson," I say with a smirk.

"Which is why you're my favorite."

He throws an arm over my shoulder and gives me a half-hug. Since he started at Walker Terraces, I don't see him as much as I used to. I know he misses Brayside and spending time with me, but he loves being the head custodian at the new building.

"Charlie hired an assistant director for Brayside." I tell him all about Ms. Appleby and what Mary Rose had to say—which was nothing good—as I let us into the building.

Grandpa waves my worries away. "Charlie knows what he's doing. He's hired everybody working there." Grandpa makes a good point. "I'm sure Ms. Appleby will work out fine once she gets used to the job."

Mom's already started dinner and Grandpa goes to see her. I head to my room with Bertie at my heels. "What the—?" I say, looking at the floor. Bits of paper are all over the place. It's like someone threw confetti at a party. "Bertie," I moan. She stares innocently back at me, and I understand the expression "puppy dog eyes." My backpack is on the floor and the math homework that used to be inside is now strewn in tiny pieces all over my floor.

The one thing she didn't chew up is the Grade 7 Edu-Trek trip information package. From what I've heard, it's the highlight of middle school. But if I want to go, Mom has to make a deposit of five hundred dollars by February 13. The total cost is twelve hundred. The permission form has been in my bag for a week, crumpled at the bottom. It isn't that I don't want to go—I do. The problem is that I'm worried about what Mom will say.

Money's been tight lately. Our rent went up and our car, which Mom needs for work, had to get some repairs. Asking for five hundred dollars right now, and seven hundred a few months later, just feels wrong.

"Austin, dinner!" Mom calls.

"Coming!" I use my hands to brush all the shredded paper under my bed. Bertie wants to help too. But her kind of helping means pouncing and snuffling through the pile of shredded paper.

"Dinnertime," Grandpa says, poking his head into my room. He raises his eyebrows. "Did Bertie do that?" he asks.

"Yeah," I say, laughing. "My dog literally ate my homework."

"Was it important?"

I shrug. "Nah, just some math." I sigh and quickly stuff the Edu-Trek form back into my bag.

Grandpa narrows his eyes at me. "Something else bugging you?"

I think about the Edu-Trek form in my bag and how much I want to go. Grandpa's not rolling in dough either, plus, Mom would hate it if I told him about the trip before her.

"No, just hungry," I say. We go to the kitchen with Bertie on our heels.

Chapter 6

Harvey

It is Sunday night. From his spot on the bed, Harvey watches Maggie. She's at her desk and still in her dance clothes, so she smells faintly of sweat. Harvey can sense her agitation. She mutters to herself and taps her pen on her desk. Finally, she picks up her phone.

"I don't know what to do!" Harvey is alert. When Maggie's voice reaches that high-pitched wail, it means there is a problem.

"Why are you stressing about this?" A girl laughs. Harvey knows Sooyeon's voice well. He likes Soo. She has long, delicate fingers that run over his back and down to his tail.

Maggie gets off her chair and comes to the bed. She flops down on it. An invitation! Harvey inches closer and licks her neck.

"Ah!" she laughs. "Harvey!" She tries to roll away, but Harvey knows it's a game. He pounces on her, tangling his paws in her hair, and licks more, covering her cheek and ear. On the phone, Soo laughs too. Finally, Maggie rolls onto her stomach. Harvey lies down and Maggie buries her fingers in his fur.

Soo's voice turns serious. "If there was an art show, would you let me chicken out?"

"No."

"You're just as good as any of the other girls. Better than most of them. And you can dance. I saw your recital."

"But can I act?"

Soo peers out at Maggie from the phone screen. "Admit it. What you're really worried about is Lexi."

Lexi. The name is familiar to Harvey. Along with another girl, Brianne, she'd been part of many sleepovers and movie nights at Maggie's house.

"She wants a lead role," Maggie says.

"So?"

Maggie slides down so she's lying with her face beside Harvey. "Things are already tense. I don't want to make them worse."

"If they're already tense, who cares if you beat her for a role! Besides, you have a major advantage."

"My hair," Maggie sighs. She takes a tendril and lets it curl around her finger.

"You of all people should play Annie."

The girls talk for a few more minutes before hanging up. Maggie puts her nose right beside Harvey's. He is starting to drift off. "What should I do, Harvs?" she asks. "The deadline to sign up for the musical is tomorrow. Would I make a good Annie?"

Harvey meets Maggie's gaze. He doesn't know the answer. In fact, Harvey is unable to think about anything except the here and now. Her warm breath tickles his nose. He reaches out his tongue and dabs her chin with it.

"Thank you," Maggie says.

Then he rolls over because in this here and now, he'd like a belly rub.

Chapter 7

Maggie

Maggie marches into school, determined. She stops at her locker to put away her coat and backpack and goes to find Sooyeon. "I'm doing it!" she announces. Sooyeon falls in step and the two girls walk purposefully to the bulletin board outside of the theater.

When they get there, Maggie's heart sinks. All of the thirty-two audition slots are full. She waited too long. Her dreams are dashed.

"Look!" Soo points out where someone's name is scribbled out. "There's technically only thirty-one slots filled."

Maggie raises her pen. Beside the scribbled-out name she adds hers: Maggie MacDonald.

Soo grins at her and holds out her hand for their secret shake, which is a series of small, intricate fist bumps, followed by finger waggles. Lexi and Brianne have moved past secret handshakes and onto bigger things, like hanging out at Tubby's with the popular seventh-grade girls and rolling up the waistbands of their skirts. Maggie is happy with the length of her skirt. It's January in Winnipeg, and the temperature is often cold enough to freeze fingers, noses, ears, and anything else not bundled properly. Legs included.

"What are you going to sing?"

"Everyone has to sing the same song," Maggie tells her. "And there's a piece of choreography we learn too, and a passage to memorize."

"Sounds very professional. Mrs. Alvarez isn't messing about." Every so often, Maggie is reminded that Soo only moved to Canada a couple of years ago. Her English tutor in Korea was British and sometimes phrases like "messing about" sneak in, along with a slight British accent.

"What if I embarrass myself?" Maggie asks.

"You won't!"

"You sound like Mrs. Fradette," Maggie says, which makes Sooyeon grin. She's met Mrs. Fradette a few times and takes Maggie's comment as a compliment.

"Did you get a spot?" Lexi asks, sidling up to Maggie. She's peering at the list with interest. Maggie notices her name is in one of the first spaces, indicating that she was in the line-up of girls waiting when Mrs. Alvarez posted it on Friday.

"Just now." Maggie points out her name.

A flicker of irritation crosses Lexi's face, but she recovers quickly. "That's lucky!" Then, in typical Lexi fashion, adds, "You shouldn't have waited so long."

Maggie nods. The way Lexi talks to her makes her feel like a small child, even though they have known each other since they were in first grade together.

"She should audition for Miss Hannigan," Soo whispers to Maggie as Lexi walks away. Maggie bites back a smile. There *are* some similarities between her former best friend and the nasty Miss Hannigan, who does everything she can to keep the girls at her orphanage miserable.

Chapter 8

Austin

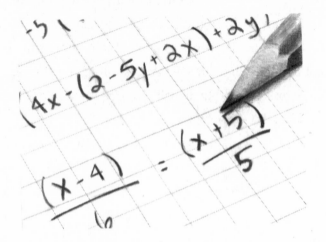

Bertie woke me up way too early, and I'm still groggy when I get to school. I have math first period. "Get out your homework," Mrs. Becker says. She winds her way up and down the rows of desks, checking to see whose work is done. And whose isn't.

"Austin?" she says.

I look up at her. Mrs. Becker is tall and has blue eyes. She keeps her hair short in a no-nonsense kind of way, which is also how she runs our class. She's been teaching at Oscar Peterson Middle School for a long time. Her bulletin board has about thirty class photos on it, one for each year she's had a homeroom. "My dog ate it. I swear." I even hold up my phone so she can see a photo of the mayhem.

She bites back a smile. "I've heard that one before," she says. "But I appreciate the evidence." She takes out three fresh sheets of math questions and puts them on my desk. "You'll have to finish these at lunch," she says.

I nod. Mrs. Becker is tough, but fair. I'm not the world's best math student, but she's always willing to help me.

Across the aisle Amar Malik tries the same excuse. "But you believed him! Why don't you believe me?"

"Because you don't have a dog," Mrs. Becker says.

"How do you know?"

Mrs. Becker fixes him with a look. "Teacher's intuition. Should we call your mom to double check?" Amar slumps in his seat, busted. Three fresh math sheets end up on his desk too. "And here's an extra one to remind you not to lie."

"See you at lunch," he mumbles to me.

Amar's the kind of kid who doesn't go out of his way to get into trouble, but it finds him anyhow. As Mrs. Becker makes her way to the next aisle, Amar leans over. "I didn't know you had a dog."

"I got her a couple of months ago. She's still a puppy." There's a lot more to the story than that. Harvey's the one who found Bertie in an alley, but it was Maggie who convinced my mom to adopt her. Maggie also arranged for all the Brayside residents to donate some money for her food and vet bills. It was the nicest thing anyone's ever done for me.

"What kind is she?"

"Part Beagle, we think. And maybe Jack Russell. She's a rescue so we aren't sure."

"I want a dog, but everyone in my family is allergic."

"Some dogs are hypoallergenic," I say. "So people with allergies can have them—"

Amar cuts me off. "They're allergic to the work, is what I mean." He grins. Amar has shaggy brown hair and brown eyes. He bought a Blue Jays hoodie with the money he got for Eid last year and wears it almost every day. He'd talk non-stop about baseball if I let him.

At the front of the room, Mrs. Becker asks for silence. "Does anyone have their Edu-Trek permission forms?" she asks. A few kids bring them up. I slouch lower in my seat.

"You going?" Amar asks.

"Still thinking about it," I say.

"I can't wait! A week of no school! My brother and sisters had so much fun. We go to a water park and stay at a haunted hotel in Quebec City." He doesn't have to tell me about all the cool stuff we'd get to do. I'd pored over the itinerary. I knew all about the tour of Niagara Falls, the Biodôme in Montreal, and the Hockey Hall of Fame in Toronto. "And we get to go to a Jays game! They're playing the Marlins!" Amar tilts his head. "Do you have a roommate?"

I hesitate. There's no point in asking someone to share a room when I don't know if I can go.

"If you already made plans—" Amar starts.

"No, I didn't," I say quickly. "I just haven't decided about the trip yet...."

"Why wouldn't you go?" Amar frowns at me.

I feel a blush rise up my neck. "Just cuz...." I fumble for an answer. "I might be going somewhere else that week. Camping. With my mom." I regret the lie as soon as I say it.

Amar gives me a funny look. I don't blame him. Who picks camping with family over a class trip out East? Someone without the money, that's who.

"I have time to decide," I say. "The deposit's not due for a couple of weeks."

"I can't promise I won't have found another roommate," Amar says, then breaks into a grin. "Kidding!" He reaches across and gives my arm a friendly punch.

"Mr. Malik!" Mrs. Becker says from the front. "Are you ready to learn?"

"Totally!" he says enthusiastically. As soon as she turns away, he smirks at me.

I have to admit, sharing a room with Amar would be a lot of fun. I just have to figure out how to convince Mom it's worth twelve hundred dollars.

Chapter 9

Maggie

A meeting is called at lunch the next day for everyone who signed up to audition for *Annie*. Thirty-two girls find spots on theater risers. Brianne and Lexi are there in a pack of five girls, the same ones they sit with in the cafeteria.

"Girls, let's get started." Mrs. Alvarez has a mass of dark, curly hair. It is usually pulled into a messy updo with a pencil or two sticking out of it. The musical theater students are used to watching Mrs. Alvarez pat her head looking for one to pull out. "I want to go over the audition procedure."

As Mrs. Alvarez explains, Maggie gets a flutter of excitement in her stomach. At St. Ambrose, two musicals are held each year: one for the senior school and then one for the middle school. In early December, Maggie watched *The Wizard of Oz*. It was so professional! She had no idea this many talented girls went to her school. When Mrs. Alvarez announced that auditions would be held for the middle-school show, Maggie knew she wanted to try out, but then doubts started to trickle in. She'd never acted before and had no experience singing in front of a crowd. What if she made a fool of herself?

"Form a line," Mrs. Alvarez says, "and pick up your audition package. You'll try out in the order you signed up."

"What are you trying out for?" Brianne asks, coming up beside Maggie. She already has an audition package in her hands.

Maggie knows whatever comes out of her mouth will go right to Lexi's ears. "I'd be happy with any role," she says. There's no point in ruffling feathers this early in the process.

Brianne nods. "Yeah. Most of the leads go to the eighth graders."

"How about you?"

"Oh, I'll probably just go for one of the orphans. Lexi's the one who really wants a lead."

Of course. "Well, good luck."

Mrs. Alvarez highlights Maggie's name on the audition list. "I was hoping you'd audition," she says, handing her a package

"You were?"

Mrs. Alvarez nods. "Of course! You're doing a great job in our musical theater class. I'd love to have you in our show this year."

Maggie is almost breathless with delight when she sits down. Maybe she has a chance after all.

Chapter 10

Harvey

All afternoon, Harvey has been perched on the couch, looking out the front window and waiting for Maggie. As soon as he spots her, he races to the back door. Harvey's joy at their reunion is unbridled. He licks her hand, jumps up, and spins. His antics are rewarded by Maggie's laughter and a good scratch right on his rump.

Usually when she comes home, Maggie's first stop is the kitchen for a snack, but not today. She shouts a quick hello to her mom and sisters and runs to her room, taking the steps two at a time. Harvey follows close behind. Clearly, there is something important to do, and Harvey doesn't want to be left out.

"Know what this is, Harvey?" Maggie asks, pulling something out of her backpack. "An audition package!" He joins her on the bed, listening attentively as Maggie begins speaking in a loud whisper. Her voice is different. It doesn't sound like his Maggie at all. "Pipe down, all of you. Do you want Hannigan to hear you?" Maggie looks around the room as if someone else is there. Harvey looks too, but sees no one.

Maggie continues, her voice changing. She pauses and stands up, gesturing. Harvey tilts his head, not understanding this new game. When her words turn angry, Harvey shrinks back, ears pinned down. Has he done something wrong?

Maggie sees him and bursts out laughing. "It's okay, Harvey! I'm not mad at you. I'm practicing." She slides back onto the bed and kisses the top of his head.

Harvey settles, relieved. "Ready for the song?" she asks and fiddles with her phone. Music plays and Maggie begins to sing. Her voice swells with the song. Harvey watches her take deep inhalations and open her mouth wide to let the sound pour out.

Harvey is so caught up that when she finishes and holds her hands up wide, he jumps off the bed and runs to her, panting with excitement.

Chapter 11

Austin

When I get to Brayside after school on Tuesday, a few of the residents are in the games room. As soon as I walk in, I know something's up. "Everything okay?" I ask.

Mrs. O'Brien shakes her head. "Alice went to the hospital this morning."

"What happened?" Now that I think about it, it's been a while since I saw Mrs. Kowalski.

"Her cold got worse on the weekend, and this morning she couldn't get out of bed." Mrs. O'Brien looks at Miss Lin and Mr. Singh. "Bob got Louise, and they called 911." The Kowalskis are one of the few couples at Brayside; married for over sixty years. "I took him some muffins just after lunch and asked if he wanted to play cards. He said he needed to wait to hear from the hospital."

"Why didn't he go with her?" I ask.

"And sit in that germ-infested waiting room for hours? No thank you!" Mr. Singh says. He makes a good point, but not knowing how Mrs. K is doing would be tough.

I wish Grandpa were here. He and Mr. K are close. When Mr. K first moved in, he'd putter in Grandpa's basement workshop, building shoe racks and bookshelves. Mrs. O'Brien must be thinking the same thing.

"I bet he'd love a visit from Phillip. We haven't seen him in ages," she says.

"I'll see if he can come by on the weekend."

"That'd be nice. Tell him I have some cookies waiting for him in the freezer," Mrs. O'Brien says. "Double chocolate chunk."

Mr. Santos bursts into the games room, waving today's newspaper in the air. He points it at me. "Just the person I was looking for." As usual, he's got the paper open to the crossword puzzle. "Reggie's a.k.a," he reads out loud.

One Reggie comes to mind, and that's Grandpa's favorite baseball player, Reggie Diggs. *A.k.a.* means also known as. "Digger?" I suggest. "Or the Digger."

Mr. Santos grabs his pencil and writes in the letters. "A-ha! That fits, and that makes this one Desdemona!"

"I better get started on some chores. Keep me posted on Mrs. K," I say as I leave the games room. I hope whatever sent her to the hospital isn't serious.

Even though Grandpa doesn't work here anymore, I still come by a few days a week to help out. I know Isaac appreciates it—he's got enough on his plate learning about the mechanics of the building. Washing some windows, patching nicks in the wall, and unclogging a drain are no big deal. Plus, as weird as it sounds, hanging out with the residents is fun. I wouldn't admit that to too many people, but it's true. Today though, the news about Mrs. K hangs over my head and so does something else—Edu-Trek.

As I was leaving school, Amar asked if I'd made a decision about the class trip. I didn't have the heart to tell him the truth, so I said "Not yet." I still don't know how I'm going to come up with the deposit, never mind the balance in a couple of months.

Isaac always writes the To-Do List on the dry-erase board hanging on the back of his office door. Today there are only two jobs: oil a squeaky hinge in Mrs. Gelman's suite and replace a few burned-out lightbulbs in the dining room.

I look around for the WD-40 I need to fix the hinge. Grandpa kept things neat and tidy, but Isaac doesn't. Every surface is cluttered with stuff. One of the desk drawers is open and right on top is an envelope. Money peeks out the opening. Not just one bill, either. *What the heck?* I pull it out to check. Sure enough, there's a bunch of twenty-dollar bills.

There's at least two-hundred dollars. Maybe more. My heart pounds hard in my chest. It wouldn't cover the whole deposit, but it'd make a dent in it. A clatter in the furnace room makes me jump. I drop the envelope and spin around. "Isaac?" My voice cracks. I thought he'd gone for the day.

A woman in blue coveralls carries a toolbox in one hand and a clipboard in the other. "He left about an hour ago. I was just doing the annual inspection."

I breathe a sigh of relief. The woman writes a note on an invoice. "You must be Austin. He said you'd be coming by. Can you make sure he gets this?"

"Yeah, sure," I say, taking the paper. She leaves and I put it in the middle of the desk, under a coffee container of tools. I stare at the envelope sitting in the drawer. What if that repair person had seen it? Or someone doing laundry? Isaac doesn't lock his office. Anyone who works at Brayside could have snatched the money from the drawer. My fingers start to tingle, and before I can think twice, I pick it up.

Louise is at the nurses' desk. Her hair has been freshly braided and it looks good. I tell her so as I pass her the envelope of money. "Isaac left it on his desk," I say.

"What is it?" She peeks inside and her eyes widen. "My goodness. What's he doing leaving so much cash lying around? Honestly, that man would forget his head if it wasn't attached to his neck."

I get a weird tickle in my throat. I don't want to think about how tempted I was to take it.

"I'll put it somewhere safe till he can come back and get it." I watch as she uses a key on the lanyard around her neck to open the locked drawer by the computer. She puts the envelope on top of some papers and closes the drawer. "Was there something else?" she asks.

I look at her, sure guilt is written all over my face. "No," I stammer and head to Mrs. Gelman's suite. I know I did the right thing, but that doesn't mean it was easy.

Chapter 12

Harvey

It's been a week since Harvey's last visit to Brayside, but since time means nothing to Harvey, he couldn't say if it has been seven months, or seven days. All he knows is that inside the building are people who care for him. Best of all, there are new smells to investigate. Just like last time, Harvey leaps out of the car as soon as Maggie lets him and waits at the sliding doors for her to catch up.

There's a chorus of greetings from the residents sitting in the foyer. Harvey goes to visit each one. First there's Mrs. Fradette, who gives excellent under-the-chin scratches. Then Miss Lin, who crochets her own slippers. Harvey would love to tear them off her feet and rip them to shreds, especially the pompoms. Finally he goes to Mr. Singh, perched on his Cobra GT4, and is rewarded with a pat on the head.

Usually the old people encourage him to run between them, but not today. They are deep in conversation. Harvey reads their cues that now is the not the time to play. He sits, obedient, at Maggie's feet.

"She's not wasting any time," Miss Lin says quietly.

"I didn't realize Brayside had so many safety hazards," Mr. Singh whispers. "Charlie never mentioned anything."

"What's going on?" Maggie asks.

"Ms. Appleby told a few of us she'll be making changes around here," Mrs. Fradette says.

"Changes?" Maggie sounds worried.

"She's implementing safety protocols," Mrs. Fradette says.

From out of the corner of Harvey's eye, he spots movement. A woman is walking toward them.

Mrs. Fradette clears her throat and they fall silent. Ms. Appleby marches over. "How often does your dog come to Brayside?"

Harvey senses the change in Maggie and shifts closer to her. There is something about his new woman that has put everyone on edge.

"He could come every day," Mrs. Fradette pipes up. "We're always happy to see Harvey."

The woman's voice is tight and her words clipped. "In the

future, you'll need to get my permission to bring the dog."

"You mean *Harvey*," Mr. Singh corrects.

"I can't have him showing up anytime. It's not good for the residents."

Miss Lin and Mr. Singh don't say anything. Even Mrs. Fradette is speechless, but only for a moment. "I think we know what's good for us," she snaps.

Ms. Appleby turns to Mrs. Fradette. When she speaks, her voice is soft and firm. "My job is to make sure you are cared for in the best way possible. Having a dog on the property is a safety concern. What if it bites someone? Or its leash gets tangled around a walker? It might prevent the nurses from doing their job properly. I'll allow the dog to stay today, but in the future you'll need to ask permission twenty-four hours in advance, and give me a list of what locations the dog will visit."

Mrs. Fradette shakes her head at Ms. Appleby's departing back. "She's turning Brayside Retirement Villa into Brayside Retirement Prison."

There's more talk among the people, but Harvey has caught a whiff of something. He puts his nose to the carpet and sniffs. He follows the scent farther along the baseboards but is forced to stop when he reaches the dining room doors. They are shut and there is no way inside. Confounded, he sits down. Harvey, like all Westies, is both stubborn and patient. He will wait as long as he has to for the doors to open so his investigation can continue.

Chapter 13

Maggie

Maggie had intended to tell Mrs. Fradette all about Friday's audition. It had gone better than expected, and Mrs. Alvarez had beamed at her when she hit the last long note in her audition song. The cast list would be posted online Sunday morning and Maggie felt confident that even if she didn't get a lead, she'd definitely have one of the larger secondary roles.

But sitting in the games room with the residents made all thought of the musical fly from her mind. It wasn't just because of the way Ms. Appleby had treated Harvey, although that was bothersome. It was the news that Mrs. Kowalski was still in the hospital.

"Is she getting any better?" Maggie asks.

Behind her thick glasses, Mrs. Fradette's eyes turn sad. "No."

Instinctively, Maggie reaches out for Harvey, but her dog isn't at her feet anymore. "Harvey," she calls, spotting him by the dining room doors. He gives an excited whimper. It's the same noise he makes at home when he's spotted a squirrel in the yard and wants someone to let him out. "You can't go in there!" Maggie scolds.

Chef Miguel's dining room is like a five-star restaurant. There are linen tablecloths and fresh flowers on each table. The daily menu makes Maggie's mouth water. She can't imagine what he'd do if he found Harvey poking around in there.

"A visit from Harvey might cheer Bob up," Miss Lin suggests.

"Good idea! Show Ms. Appleby that Harvey does important work around here." Mr. Singh nods from his scooter.

If Maggie wants to keep visiting with Harvey, proving to Ms. Appleby that her dog serves a useful purpose is a great idea. She says good-bye to everyone in the games room and promises to come back later. "Let's go, Harvs," she says and walks down the hallway. "Time to visit Mr. Kowalski." And in her head she silently adds, *while you still can*.

Maggie knocks on Mr. Kowalski's door and Harvey sits, waiting. He looks up at Maggie with his brown eyes and then turns back to the door. Maggie can't help but smile. She can always count on Harvey.

When the door opens it isn't Mr. Kowalski, but Austin, who's standing there. Just like always, Harvey greets him as if it's been months since their last visit. Maggie can see Mr. Kowalski. He's sitting at the kitchen table and the smell of freshly brewed coffee fills the air. Austin moves aside as Harvey barrels through and runs to Mr. Kowalski.

"Hi, Mr. Kowalski!" Maggie says, smiling.

Mr. Kowalski says hello, but his attention is on Harvey.

"We have a problem," Maggie whispers to Austin as she steps inside the suite, "and her name is Appleby."

Five minutes later, mugs of coffee are in front of all three of them. It's decaf because of Mr. Kowalski's blood pressure. Austin's and Maggie's have more milk and sugar than coffee. The warmth of the drink feels right in his apartment, where they're surrounded by knickknacks and family photos.

As Maggie explains what happened with Ms. Appleby in the foyer, Austin's mouth hangs open. "Twenty-four hours' notice? Why? Harvey's been coming here for months."

"Mrs. Fradette says she's turning Brayside into a prison." Maggie hates the idea of the vibrant group of old people living with so many rules.

"If she's worried about a well-behaved dog like Harvey, what's she going to think about Bertie?" Austin asks.

Mr. Kowalski slurps his coffee and shakes his head.

"Wait till I tell Alice," he harrumphs.

"How's Mrs. Kowalski doing?" Maggie asks, hoping her condition isn't as bad as Mrs. Fradette thinks.

"No change," he says. "My daughter's coming by soon, and we'll go over." Mr. Kowalski's eyes fall on a photo of the two of them. "It's quiet around here without her. I didn't realize how much she talked. I keep turning on the TV just for the noise." He gives a sad smile. "I sure do miss her."

Austin leans across the table and meets Mr. Kowalski's eyes. "She's gonna make it through this, Mr. K."

Mr. Kowalski gives Austin a brave smile and nods.

Chapter 14

Austin

Mom's making pancakes by the time I get out of the shower on Sunday morning.

"What time were you up?" she asks. Bertie is sleeping in her favorite spot—the corner of the couch that faces the window. She looks very comfortable.

"Don't ask," I grumble. After waking me up at 5 A.M. to play, Bertie went back to sleep. I tried to, but then I got thinking about Edu-Trek, the cost, Isaac's money, which I still couldn't believe I'd considered stealing, and Mrs. Kowalski, and it became impossible.

I also need to come clean with Amar. He's been sending

me almost daily texts telling me how epic the trip is going to be and how much fun it will be to share a room.

Mom gives me a sympathetic smile as I slump down at the kitchen table. "Any plans for the day?" she asks.

"I'll probably go to Brayside later," I say. "What about you?"

She sighs. "More job hunting."

Mom puts a plate of pancakes in front of me. I see the dark circles under her eyes. It doesn't look like she slept much either. "I could get a job. Like delivering papers, or babysitting, or dog-walking." We've had this discussion before.

Mom says what she always says. "You're already busy with school and Brayside. Plus, Bertie needs your attention. She's still a puppy." She looks over at Bertie, who snores in her sleep and rolls over. I take another bite of my syrupy pancakes, but they don't taste so sweet anymore. "I know you want to help, Austin, but I'll get something. It's just taking longer than I thought."

As I pack up for Brayside, Bertie follows me around the apartment. She watches me with her big eyes. I get a twinge of guilt for leaving her, but Mom is home today, so she won't be alone.

"I'll be back soon," I tell her. When I shut the door after me, I hear Bertie whining on the other side. The whimpers follow me all the way down the hallway. I pause with my hand on the elevator button.

I know I can't take her. Ms. Appleby was at Brayside yesterday and made a comment about coming back today.

It's like she doesn't know the meaning of the word *weekend*. Bertie's not as well behaved as Harvey. If she gets into trouble, Ms. Appleby might make a no-dogs rule. The residents would hate that. Maggie would hate that. *I'd* hate that.

I take a deep breath and press the down button, trying to shut out the sounds of my puppy's cries.

I'm still thinking about Bertie when I get to Brayside. Charlie is just leaving and I pass him in the entrance. "Can't stay away?" I joke.

Charlie has his briefcase tucked under one arm and chuckles. "No, no. Just needed to pick up some files. Walker Terraces is keeping your grandpa and me busy enough. It's been nice to pass the reins for this place over to Hilary," he says.

I wish I could tell him what everyone else thinks about that, but it's not my place. Besides, maybe Grandpa is right and she'll loosen up once she gets settled. I say good-bye to Charlie and take a deep breath. Delicious smells are coming out of the dining room.

Sundays are busy because lots of families come to visit. Chef Miguel does a brunch buffet in the dining room, so the residents can invite guests. It's nice for the ones who have family nearby, but some, like Miss Lin, spend Sundays alone. I go to her suite first for a couple hands of poker. Thanks to Mrs. Fradette, Texas hold'em has replaced bridge at Brayside.

Miss Lin wins almost every hand of poker. She looks all sweet and innocent, but she's a bit of a card shark. Good thing we were playing with Bingo chips and not real money.

I'm chatting with Artie at the nurses' station when Isaac arrives. He's not in his coveralls. In fact, he's dressed up kind of fancy. His hair is slicked back and under his jacket I can see a tie knotted at his neck. He's got on shiny shoes and dress pants.

Artie whistles. "You clean up good!"

Isaac grins. "On my way to my niece's birthday party," he says. He turns to me. "Heard you found the cash on my desk." He shakes his head like he can't believe he left it lying around.

"Yeah, the other day when the furnace was getting checked. I didn't want anyone to take it." I gulp. That's mostly the truth.

"I figured it was safer to leave it locked up here. It's for my niece's birthday. I want her parents to start one of those savings accounts, like for university."

That explains all the cash, but now I feel worse for almost keeping it.

Isaac checks the time on his phone. "I better grab it. Late as usual," he mutters under his breath. When Louise put it away, she used a key on her lanyard to open the drawer. Artie tries all his keys, but none fit. He tries them all a second time and then passes the lanyard to Isaac.

I wish I'd just left the money on his desk. Or better yet, never found it at all.

"I could bust it open," Isaac says, giving the drawer a jiggle.

Artie shoots him a look. "Have fun explaining that to Mary Rose."

"Guess I'll just write an I.O.U to my niece," Isaac says with a sigh. He doesn't look so freshly scrubbed anymore. In fact, thanks to me, he looks totally disgruntled.

"Sorry, Isaac," I say.

He shrugs. "Not your fault. I shouldn't have left it lying around. You did the right thing." His phone rings. Isaac answers it, and I hear rushed apologies about being late for the party as he heads for the door.

I grab a duster and swipe it across the window ledges and end tables in the foyer. Brayside is clean as a whistle, but I'm willing to do anything to take away the guilty feeling that's settled in my gut. I'm dusting the shelves behind the reception desk when Mr. K arrives a few minutes later. Dropped off by his daughter, he walks through the sliding glass doors looking lost, as if he doesn't know how he wound up back at Brayside.

"Hey, Mr. K," I say, going over. "How are you?"

He snaps back to himself when he looks at me. *It was just a momentary blip*, I think, relieved. Seeing Mrs. K in the hospital probably has him shook up. Mr. K takes in the fireplace. Lately the reception staff have been making sure a fire is going. It takes the wintery chill out of the air and makes the foyer feel cozy.

"The fire sure is nice," he says.

"We could sit out here," I suggest. The dining room is almost empty now that the brunch buffet is over. The residents usually relax in their suites on Sunday afternoon, worn out from visiting.

Mr. K hangs up his jacket on the coatrack by the door. He got dressed up to go to the hospital. With a loud exhalation, he sits down on the couch. "How's Mrs. K?" I ask.

He frowns. "She's not getting worse, so I guess that's something." She's been in the hospital for a week now. "In all our years of marriage, we've never been apart this long."

"You must miss her."

Mr. K nods and he gets a faraway look in his eye.

"How'd you meet Mrs. K?" I ask. Just as I suspected, my question rouses him a little. Old people love reminiscing.

"Kind of a funny story, actually. I met Alice when we were eleven. She was visiting her cousins in Neepawa. It was 1942. The RAF flying school had just opened up, because of the war.

"What's RAF?"

"Royal Air Force. Us boys liked to go down to the airfield and watch the Tiger Moths zipping through the sky. Tiger Moths were bi-planes, the kind with wings one on top of the other." He pauses for a minute, remembering. "And because pilots had come from all over to train, every couple of weeks there'd be a dance. It was mainly to keep the airmen entertained, but the whole town went. That's where I first saw Alice."

Maybe it's the fire crackling behind him, or thinking about his childhood, but some of the worry lines disappear as Mr. K talks.

Chapter 15

Harvey

Harvey has just drifted off when he's startled awake by Maggie slapping her laptop shut. He looks up at her, curious about what is wrong.

"No, no, no," Maggie moans. She covers her face with her hands and makes little gasping noises.

Harvey is now very curious and sits up. Wanting to know more, he stretches his nose closer to her face. Salty tears wet her cheeks. Her shoulders shake with sobs. Harvey springs into action, giving her kisses and licking away her tears, comforting her the only way he knows how.

There is a knock on the door. Harvey jumps down and

is relieved to see Maggie's mom poke her head in the door. "What's wrong?" she asks.

"The cast list came out." Maggie sobs. "I'm an—an—" She can't get the words out. Maggie's mom sits on the edge of her bed and rubs her daughter's shoulders. Harvey takes his position, guarding Maggie.

"It can't be that bad," Maggie's mom says.

"An understudy!" Maggie finally spits out.

The comforting hand momentarily freezes, but Maggie's mom makes a quick recovery. "Well, understudies are very important. You never know what might happen the day of a show."

Maggie flings herself over to face her mother. Harvey repositions himself so he can see both of them. "It's humiliating! I don't even have a speaking role. I'm in the *chorus*!"

The high-pitched tone of Maggie's voice worries Harvey.

"At least you have something. I'm sure lots of girls didn't get any role at all."

Maggie buries her head in her pillow. Harvey moves over so he can lie next her. Her mom pats Maggie's back consolingly. "It's not the end of the world."

"It feels like it," Maggie says.

Chapter 16

Austin

I like how Mr. K is telling his story, so I don't rush him.

"I was feeling pretty proud of myself because that summer I'd got my first job as a telegram boy," he says.

"What's a telegram boy?" I ask.

"Back then, important messages came in as morse code over a telegraph. The operator decoded them and typed them up, and then I delivered them. I got paid a dollar eighty a week."

I smirk at how little money that is.

"Don't laugh. That was enough for me to buy the two things that mattered most—comics and fishing line."

He chuckles under his breath. "Plus, I could pay my own way into the dances."

I try to picture Mr. K on a dance floor, but can't do it. "Were you a good dancer?"

He snorts. "I couldn't dance to save my life, at least not in the beginning. Back then, every song had a certain type of dance that went with it. The emcee called it out, and you had to know the dance if you were going to ask a young lady to join you."

"That sounds like a lot of pressure," I say.

"It was, especially for a kid with no sisters or girl cousins to teach me. But once I saw Alice, I was desperate to learn. Now there was a girl who could move. She looked like Ginger Rogers. None of the other girls could dance anywhere near as good." Mr. K's eyes twinkle. "I was too shy to talk to her, but I figured it was fate when one of my first telegram deliveries was for the Davidsons, the cousins she was staying with.

"Before I set out, the postmaster, Mr. Erstwhile, gave me my instructions. Any telegram in a white envelope with a purple Commonwealth seal was to be given to the person it was addressed to. I wasn't to slip it in the mail slot like the others. 'And you might want to ask a neighbor to go with you,' he said.

"'Why's that?' I asked.

"'In case they faint.'

"'Faint, sir?' I asked. Mr. Erstwhile nodded, and that was when I realized what I'd got myself into. Some of the telegrams I was delivering were from the war office, telling a wife her husband—or a mother her son—had been killed."

"Oh," I say, understanding. "And you had to take one to Mrs. K's family?"

Mr. K nods. "Her aunt. I knew Mr. Davidson was in the military, but I couldn't remember if he was overseas or not. My brother, Andrew, had enlisted, and as much as I missed him, his letters made the war sound like a great adventure. The whole way to the Davidson's house, I was sweating. I thought about turning back a few times, but I couldn't quit on my first day." The smile that's been in his voice fades away. "I did as Mr. Erstwhile said and waited at the door for Mrs. Davidson to answer. I hoped Alice wasn't there. I didn't want her thinking of me poorly if the telegram was bad news.

"Mrs. Davidson came to the door. She looked at me and what I had in my hands. Her face got still. 'Give it to me,' she said. I watched as she ripped it open."

"And?"

"It was good news. Her husband had received a promotion. She even gave me a nickel tip." Mr. K laughs.

I breathe out a sigh of relief for Mr. K. "Close one."

"It was. As I pedaled away, I glanced back." There's a twinkle in Mr. K's eyes. "Who do you think was peering at me through the living room window?"

"Mrs. K."

Mr. K nods happily. The story might be from 1942, but hearing him now, it doesn't feel so long ago.

Chapter 17

Maggie

Before leaving for Brayside, Maggie goes over the cast list, checking it for the tenth time.

What went wrong with her audition? Mrs. Alvarez had seemed happy. Soo had heard her practice and had been as confident as Maggie that she'd get a role. Were the other girls that much better than her?

The worst part will be telling Mrs. Fradette. She's been so confident in Maggie's talent and excited to see her perform. Maggie gets a knot in her stomach at the thought of disappointing her.

To Maggie's chagrin, Ms. Appleby is at the front reception

desk when she walks in. *Doesn't she ever take a day off?* Maggie wonders. She's glad she clipped Harvey's leash onto his collar, because once inside, he spots Austin on the couch with Mr. Kowalski. Harvey strains on the leash, eager to see them both. Most people would be delighted to see a dog this happy to greet someone, but not Ms. Appleby. Her face hardens into a frown. Maggie plasters a smile on her face. *Acting!* She silently declares. "Hi, Ms. Appleby. I hope it's okay Harvey's here. I sent an e-mail, just like you asked."

Ms. Appleby's expression doesn't change. "I have something to show you," she says.

Maggie glances at Harvey, who's got his front paws on Mr. K's knees. When she gets to the reception desk, Ms. Appleby hands her a paper. "I've made a few changes to the safety protocols at Brayside," she says. "Starting with pet visits."

"Look at this!" Maggie hisses and shoves a paper in Austin's face.

Protocol for Animal Visits to Brayside. Under the title are fifteen new rules. Number one reads, Animal Must be Leashed at All Times.

Some of the rules are obvious, like not letting Harvey in the dining room or kitchen. But others like number four, Animals Can Only be Around Three Residents at Once, and number five, Must Always be Within Arm's Length of Its Owner, are ridiculous, especially if Harvey's already on his leash.

"He's not allowed at any gatherings or special events either." Maggie fumes. "If I hadn't promised Mrs. Fradette I'd come by today, I'd just leave. How can she treat Harvey like this? He's being punished for no reason. Does she have something against all dogs? Or just Harvey?"

"He's such a sweet, little dog," Mr. Kowalski says and leans down to pat Harvey's head. "He's never given us any trouble." Maggie silently thanks Mr. Kowalski for not mentioning his slippers.

"I wish Ms. Appleby thought so." Maggie frowns and wonders if this day could get any worse. First the cast list and now rules for Harvey.

"Am I looking at Annie?" Mrs. Fradette asks. She spins Maggie around, holding her at arm's length.

Maggie opens her mouth. "Uh…well," the truth is on the tip of her tongue, but instead, "Yes!" is what pops out. Mrs. Fradette claps her hands, pulls Maggie into a congratulatory hug, and doesn't hear the second part of Maggie's answer, "Sort of."

"I knew it!" Mrs. Fradette says. "I knew you'd get it!"

Mr. Kowalski looks from one to the other, confused.

Maggie opens her mouth to admit she's not exactly the lead, but Mrs. Fradette barely pauses to take a breath. "Our Maggie is going to be the star in the St. Ambrose production of *Annie*!"

"Wow! You are?" Austin asks. "Why didn't you say something sooner?"

"Because of this!" she says, holding up the list of rules.

Ms. Appleby is no longer at the desk, so Maggie passes it to Mrs. Fradette.

Mrs. Fradette reads it quietly to herself, her eyes widening in disbelief. "Number seven: Animals Will Not Visit Residents In Their Rooms!" She pulls her mouth into a thin line. "What's she worried about?"

"I don't know!" Maggie wails.

"That Ms. Appleby can stick it in her ear!" Mrs. Fradette says huffily.

"Maybe if we talk to her and explain that the rules—" Austin suggests.

Mrs. Fradette interrupts him. "Rules, schmules! Having Harvey here isn't hurting anyone!"

That fiery determination is just what Maggie needed. Her mood shifts. With Mrs. Fradette at Brayside, Ms. Appleby and her rules don't stand a chance.

Maggie has a hard time concentrating at school the next morning. The first *Annie* rehearsal is at lunchtime. She's already heard Lexi bragging about her role. Just as Sooyeon predicted, Lexi was cast as Ms. Hannigan, one of the leads.

When the lunch bell rings, Maggie says good-bye to Sooyeon, who is going to the art room to work on sets. "Have fun," Soo says, trying to stay upbeat. Maggie gives her a half-hearted smile and continues to the theater.

"Congratulations!" A girl squeals and runs past her to Ndidi Udo, the girl who got the role of Annie. Ndidi's hair isn't red, it's black, but it is curly like Annie's. Other girls are congratulating her, and Maggie's insides twist. Not with jealousy, exactly. *Wanting* is a better word. Maybe *regret* that it's not her they're congratulating.

"Hi, Mags," Lexi says, waving as if they're still best friends. Maggie tries not to react to Lexi's smug expression.

Brianne looks genuinely pleased for both the girls. "It's cool you're the understudy! That's basically like being the backup lead!"

Lexi doesn't waste the opportunity to point out Brianne's error. "It's not *like* being a backup. It is a backup, Bri." The word backup cuts right through Maggie.

Brianne shrugs. "I think it's great. I mean, it's a big responsibility."

"Thanks," Maggie says, mustering as much goodwill as she can.

Maggie has just sat down when Mrs. Alvarez calls her over. "I made a mistake on the cast list."

Maggie's heart races. It's just like she hoped! Was there a mix-up with another girl? Maybe she's meant to be Annie and Ndidi is the understudy. If that's true, she won't have to come clean with Mrs. Fradette.

"You aren't the understudy for Annie."

Maggie's face breaks into a grin, anticipating good news.

"You're the understudy for *all* the leads."

Maggie's breath catches in her throat.

"I know you were probably hoping for a different role. But being an understudy is so, so important. It's a huge task. When I reviewed the auditions, you were the one with the most versatility."

Maggie nods. She knows Mrs. Alvarez is giving her a compliment, but if everyone stays healthy, she'll never set foot on center stage.

Chapter 18

Austin

Mr. K's story about being a telegram boy got me thinking. Even though Mom says I'm too busy to get a job, there's no harm in trying. Working at Brayside would be great, but there's no way it'll happen. Charlie's cheap, and Ms. Appleby's a stickler for rules. Instead, I put up a sign in our building.

Responsible Dog Walker and/or Babysitter
Reasonable Rates

I add my phone number on those little tear-away strips at the bottom. I do the math. I'd have to walk a lot of dogs and sit a lot of babies to make anywhere close to twelve hundred dollars.

There is one other option that I've been avoiding; charity.

I stop by my homeroom at the end of the day. Mrs. Becker is at her desk marking papers.

"Excuse me, Mrs. Becker," I say, super polite. "Can I talk to you for a second?"

She puts down her pen and waves me in. "What's up?"

"It's about Edu-Trek," I say.

She nods for me to continue. "I was just wondering… um…if there's any way to… lower the cost."

Mrs. Becker frowns. "It is a little steep, isn't it?"

I nod. "I was thinking, maybe I could work it off? By helping Mr. Ramillo?"

"The custodian?" Mrs. Becker asks.

"I volunteer at Brayside Retirement Villa. It's where my grandpa used to work. He taught me to do a lot of odd jobs."

Mrs. Becker considers my idea. She doesn't say no. At least not right away. "I could ask, but I'm not sure it's allowed."

My shoulders slump. So much for that idea.

"I'm sorry, Austin," Mrs. Becker says kindly when I head for the door.

"That's okay. See you tomorrow."

Like all my other ideas to make money, this one is a failure too. I kind of want to head home and see Bertie. If anyone can raise my spirits, it's her, but Isaac is expecting me. Plus, I want to check on Mr. K. I might be bummed about Edu-Trek, but that's nothing compared to what it's like for him with Mrs. K in the hospital.

My expression must give away how I'm feeling because as soon as I walk in, Mary Rose zeroes in on me and asks what's wrong. I don't want to complain. She's raising four kids on her nurse's salary; not going on a school trip isn't life or death. "Just had a long day," I say.

She tilts her head at me. "Bob's not doing great," she says. "Alice's pneumonia has spread to the other lung."

"No," I groan. Isaac's chores can wait. I head straight to the Kowalski's suite.

I wish I had Harvey with me when I knock on the door. If anyone needs a comfort animal right now, it's Mr. K. "Sorry, Austin. I'm not up for visitors," he says right away. There's a pile of dishes in the sink. A few days' worth of newspapers are scattered over the table.

"I thought I might tidy up a bit, if that's okay." Mom would faint from shock if she heard me making this offer.

Mr. K looks around as if he's noticing the mess for the first time. "Alice usually does that…." He trails off. Mr. K shuffles over to the kitchen table where he has a cup of coffee and the phone in front of him, like he's waiting for a call.

I fill the sink with water and soap. Mr. K barely moves

while I wash the dishes and straighten up. I even plump the pillows on the couch. When I'm done, his place looks more like it usually does.

"Thanks, Austin. Guess I let things go a little."

"It happens," I say. "You've got a lot on your mind."

His face falls. "Alice's condition is worse. I'm worried." He takes off his glasses and wipes his eyes.

He said he wasn't up for a visit, but there's no way I can leave now. "Mrs. K's not a quitter," I say confidently. "She's gonna get better!" His eyes are still wet as he looks across the room at their wedding photo. I think about asking him to tell me more about Neepawa. We never got to the part where he met Mrs. K, but then his phone rings.

"It's my daughter," he says. I take that as my cue.

"I'll come by tomorrow," I say, and go to the door.

I pass Mary Rose at the nurses' station on my way to the basement. I want to see if Isaac left me any chores.

"You look worse than when you came in," she says, fixing me with one of her looks—the kind that doesn't miss anything.

"Of all the residents, Mrs. K is the last one I thought would get sick."

"The best thing you or any of us can do is keep positive, Austin."

I know she's right, but it's hard, especially seeing the way Mr. K is handling things. Mary Rose goes back to rifling through a drawer.

"What are you doing?" I ask. Mary Rose always keeps the nurses' station tidy, but today it looks like a tornado blew through.

"That money of Isaac's wasn't where Louise put it. We looked, but it's gone. I thought maybe it had slipped behind the drawer." That explains the stacks of papers and file folders on the desk.

"It's a lot of money," I say, worried. *Why did I have to pick it up?* I ask myself for the hundredth time.

"The worst part is, only Louise and I have keys to this drawer, which makes us the prime suspects."

"There's no way Isaac would think you took it," I say.

"It's not him I'm worried about." She casts her eyes in the direction of Ms. Appleby's office.

Chapter 19

Maggie

M aggie has been in rehearsals every day and by the time the weekend rolls around, all she wants to do is stay home and watch Netflix.

But then on Sunday Austin sends her a text telling her that Mrs. Kowalski's pneumonia is worse and everyone's worried. Harvey sits on the floor staring at her. She knows that look. He wants to go for a walk, but it's minus bajillion outside, and going for a walk is the last thing Maggie wants to do.

"Tell you what," she says. "We'll split the difference and go to Brayside. Everyone could use a little Harvey magic."

Austin is already there when Maggie and Harvey arrive. He's chatting with Artie outside of Mr. Santos' room. They both throw a surprised look at Maggie and then at Harvey. "Did you let Ms. Appleby know he was coming?" Artie asks.

Maggie shakes her head, guiltily. "We came for Mr. K. I didn't think the protocols mattered much under the circumstances." Harvey's been visiting for such a long time, putting these rules in now seems so silly. Plus, *she* knows Harvey can help, even if Ms. Appleby doesn't.

Artie sighs. "Mr. K's been eating his meals in his suite instead of the dining room. He wants to be near the phone."

"I went to see him earlier, but he didn't answer the door," Austin adds.

"He'll come out when he's ready. We just have to be patient," Artie says.

Maggie notices Austin seems a little off too. He spends an extra-long time patting Harvey. "Everything okay with you?"

Austin gives a dispirited shrug. "My mom interviewed for a job last week. She said the interview went well, but they called on Friday to tell her she didn't get it."

"That's too bad." Maggie watches him. She knows there must be more to it.

He slides his eyes away from hers. "There's this school trip I want to go on, but it costs twelve hundred dollars...." Austin drifts off, letting Maggie put the pieces together. "There's something else too." As Austin explains about the missing money and his role in taking it to Louise, Maggie interrupts.

"You should have left it in Isaac's office."

"I know." Austin groans. And now it's gone, and Louise and Mary Rose are the only people with keys to the drawer."

"They wouldn't take it," Maggie says. "Neither would Artie, or anyone else working here."

"Except someone did take it, because it's not there."

Maggie is about to offer some consoling words when she realizes Harvey has wandered toward the dining room. He's not on his leash and is farther than an arm's length away, which breaks rules two and four. Maggie chases after him. "Good thing Ms. Appleby isn't here!"

"She wasn't supposed to be here last Sunday either, but she showed up. Charlie keeps telling Grandpa what a hard worker she is and how lucky he is to have found her," Austin shakes his head as they walk to the games room, Harvey in tow. "He loves that she stays late and comes in on weekends. He said hiring her was like getting two employees for the price of one. But all she's doing is making up rules and walking around with that clipboard. She hasn't gotten to know any of the residents. She barely talks to the nurses, except to boss them around or question them on things."

Maggie doesn't spend as much time at Brayside as Austin, but she knows there's more to running a place like this than making up rules.

It's no use trying to hold Harvey back once they get to the

games room. All his favorites are in there. Mrs. Fradette and Mrs. O'Brien are on the couch. Across from them, Miss Lin is sitting in a chair, and beside her, on his scooter, is Mr. Singh. Maggie lets go of the leash, and Harvey races ahead to a round of surprised greetings.

"There she is! There's our Annie!" Mrs. Fradette says. Maggie forces a smile. She intended to tell Mrs. Fradette the truth about being the understudy, but now isn't the time—not with everyone here.

"We didn't know you were coming," Mrs. O'Brien says. "I'd have saved you a blueberry muffin." A plate with only crumbs sits on the coffee table in front of them.

"I had two," Mr. Singh admits. "They were delicious."

Mrs. Fradette has a notepad on her lap. "What are you doing?" Maggie asks.

"Planning the Valentine's Dance," Mr. Singh says. "We have it every year. It's quite the affair. We hire a band and decorate the games room. The dining room serves a light dinner."

"The ladies wear red, and we invite all the Brayside residents. Lots of people from the second floor come. Most of them can't dance, but they like to listen to the band," Mrs. O'Brien adds.

"We're making a to-do list," Mrs. Fradette says. Her pen is

poised over the paper when she turns to Maggie. Her eyes are magnified through her thick lenses. "Margaret! You could sing for us! A song from *Annie*! Wouldn't that be lovely?"

Miss Lin, Mrs. O'Brien, and Mr. Singh all nod enthusiastically. Maggie's stomach sinks.

Artie appears at the door. He looks worried. "*Psst*, Maggie," he whispers and points behind him. "Appleby is here!"

Maggie looks at her little dog, lying at Mrs. Fradette's feet, happy to be part of the group. The idea that he would cause any kind of trouble is ridiculous. But rules are rules, and Ms. Appleby is the boss now.

Austin's face hardens with determination. "We can't let her find him," he says. "Artie! Can you distract her?" he says.

"I'll do my best."

Maggie looks around the room. There's a closet along the back wall, but hiding Harvey in there is a bad idea. He might get scared and bark. "We need to sneak him into someone's suite."

"How about Mr. K's?" Austin asks. "He might like to be part of the action."

"Yes," Mrs. O'Brien says. "That's a good idea. I know he's missing Alice. A visit from Harvey is just the thing."

Mrs. Fradette eyes the basket on Mr. Singh's scooter and springs into action. Out comes his winter scarf, newspaper, and water bottle. In goes Harvey. He squirms a little, but once the scarf is tucked around him, the basket is quite comfortable, and Harvey sits down.

"We have to cover him with something," Maggie says. She looks around the room and grabs a lace doily from under a lamp. It's the same color as Harvey, and if he stays low, Ms. Appleby might not notice him.

"We need a lookout," Mrs. Fradette says. "And someone else should go ahead to let Bob know we're coming." Austin volunteers. He peeks into the hallway and motions all clear.

Chapter 20

Austin

O kay, so a bunch of old people, especially one on a scooter, aren't exactly inconspicuous. Mr. Singh zips ahead, followed by Mrs. Fradette and Maggie, but Mrs. O'Brien needs help getting out of her chair, and Miss Lin isn't strong enough to do it. They end up erupting into giggles as Mrs. O'Brien's bottom lands back on the cushion. I abandon my lookout position and go back to help. From the games room, I can hear Ms. Appleby's voice. She and Artie are coming this way!

I hope Mr. Singh's Cobra GT4 is fast enough to get Harvey into Mr. K's room without Ms. Appleby seeing them.

"Oh, I have to show you this one," Artie says, holding up

his phone in front of Ms. Appleby's face. "Look! The nurses dressed up as elves for our Christmas tree decorating party."

Ms. Appleby pauses in the hallway in front of the games room. She isn't even trying to look interested. "Artie, I don't have time for this."

Mrs. O'Brien and Miss Lin both wince at her tone and move as quickly as they can into the hallway. Just in time, I see Mr. Singh gun it into Mr. K's room. "Hi, Artie," I say. "Hi, Ms. Appleby."

"You're here again?" she says.

"Yeah, I come here a lot."

She narrows her eyes at me. "Charlie mentioned you do repairs." Ms. Appleby holds up the clipboard in her hands and flips to a new page. She pulls out a pen and clicks it open. "What sorts of things have you fixed?"

"Uh, lots of things. Why?"

"You're not certified. Whatever you've repaired could be done incorrectly. We can't put the resident's safety at risk. An inspector from the Health Department is coming next week. I don't want any surprises."

I can't believe what she's saying. Grandpa taught me how to do things, like hanging pictures properly, patching nail holes in the walls, caulking tubs, and fixing leaky taps. He wouldn't have shown me how if he didn't trust me.

"Austin knows what he's doing," Artie says, jumping to my defense.

But Ms. Appleby makes a note on her pad. "I'll expect a list from you by next Friday. In the future, Isaac is the only one who will be doing repairs."

She clicks the pen closed and marches back toward the front desk. "Looks like Harvey's not the only one on a short leash around here," Artie mutters shaking his head.

Chapter 21

Maggie

I t's a relief when Mr. Kowalski opens the door to his suite. He looks surprised to see so many people in front of him. He also looks tired. Worrying about Mrs. Kowalski is taking a toll on him.

"Mind if we come in?" Mr. Singh says. "We have an important package." He lifts the doily up so Mr. Kowalski can see two brown eyes and a black nose peeking up at him.

"He's here on an unauthorized visit," Mrs. Fradette explains. "And Appleby showed up."

Mr. Kowalski gestures them inside and not a moment too soon, because Ms. Appleby and her clipboard are headed in their direction.

As soon as the door is shut, Maggie lifts Harvey out of the basket and puts him on the floor.

"That was a close call," Mrs. Fradette says, making herself comfortable on the couch.

"I hope she doesn't decide to do spot checks on our rooms," Mr. Singh says.

"Can she even do that?" Maggie asks.

No one answers.

Harvey is sitting at Mr. Kowalski's feet, his nose pressed against the old man's leather slippers. Mr. Kowalski ignores Harvey. He's not even paying attention to the conversation going on around him.

Mrs. Fradette gets back down to business planning the Valentine's dance. "Bob, you and Alice are in charge of decorations."

He startles at his name. "What?"

"Decorations. For the dance," Mrs. Fradette repeats.

"Oh, right. Alice will like that," he agrees, then frowns. "If she's back."

"She will be," Mrs. Fradette assures him and reaches over to pat his hand.

There's a knock at the door and everyone freezes . "Think it's her?" Mrs. Fradette asks. Maggie gets ready to scoop Harvey up and hide him. She looks at the closet near the door. Would Harvey stay quiet if she put him in there? But then she thinks, *Ms. Appleby's rules are ridiculous. If that's her at the door, it's time I told her so.*

There's another knock. "It's me," Austin says.

Maggie sighs with relief. When she opens the door, she sees that Austin has collected Mrs. O'Brien, Miss Lin, and Mr. Santos too. Mrs. Gelman is there, leaning on her walker. Artie is pushing Mrs. Gustafson's wheelchair.

The Kowalski's suite is packed with furniture on a normal day. Adding all the guests, Mrs. Gustafson's chair, and the Cobra GT4 makes it very crowded.

"Guess what Austin just told me!" Mr. Santos doesn't wait for anyone to guess before telling them. "He isn't allowed to do any more repairs! Appleby says it's too risky since he's not certified. She's taking this too far!" He raises his fist. Some of his combover flops to the wrong side.

"Risky? My fanny!" Mrs. O'Brien snaps. Normally, Maggie would have laughed to see sweet Mrs. O'Brien so fired up, but one look at Austin's face tells her there's nothing funny about this. Being able to help at Brayside makes Austin feel important. The residents depend on him.

Maggie doesn't know what, but something has to be done to ensure Brayside remains the place the residents have come to love. It's their home, and nothing Ms. Appleby does should change that.

Chapter 22

Harvey

Harvey is very comfortable lying on the floor at Mr. Kowalski's feet. The smell of salty slippers fills his nose, but when Mr. Kowalski accidentally jabs him in the side with his foot, the little terrier goes in search of a better spot.

Harvey winds his way in and out, between and through, until a distinctive scent gets his attention. He puts his nose to the ground, right along the baseboard, where the wall meets the floor. Like an invisible string, the smell reels Harvey out the door and into the hallway. Just like when he unknowingly wandered away from his home, Harvey forgets what lies behind him and focuses on what's ahead.

He blocks out all smells but the one he's focused on, taking short, quick inhalations. His black nose quivers as he trots past the suites, past the games room, and straight toward the dining room.

Chef Miguel is standing in the foyer writing out today's menu. If Harvey weren't hot on the trail of this new scent, he'd pause to greet the man covered in many layers of kitchen smells. Miguel has dark hair slicked back into a neat ponytail. He doesn't notice Harvey pass behind him, or that a dog—*a dog!*—has found its way into his dining room.

Harvey is only vaguely aware that the trail has led him into Brayside's dining room. He is too intent on following the scent to explore the large and foreign territory.

As a ratter, Harvey is single-minded in his pursuit. The term *dogged* is an accurate description, because at this moment Harvey can't let go of the scent. Instinct tells him it is a live thing. *An intruder!* The mysterious smell winds away from the baseboards and under tables and between chair legs. It zigs and zags all over the dining room. Harvey follows his nose until he finds himself blocked. *Blast that swinging kitchen door!* He can nudge it with his nose, but it is too heavy to squeeze past. If only he could get through, he is certain he could root out the source of the scent. The kitchen pulses with it.

Suddenly, a pair of hands grabs him by the collar. An arm wraps around his body and lifts him high above the floor. "Gotcha!" says a voice, triumphant.

Chapter 23

Austin

Maggie turns her head to the left and right, staring at the floor. Then she bends down to check under Mr. K's kitchen table and chairs. She doesn't have to say anything before I'm looking under furniture in the living room.

Harvey.

Our eyes go to the door. It's not open much, but enough that Harvey could have slipped out.

We bolt to the hallway. Maggie looks toward the courtyard, and I go to the front door. The best-case scenario is that someone at the reception desk found him. Worst-case scenario is that the someone is Ms. Appleby, and we're in trouble. Big time.

"He's not in the foyer," I tell Maggie when she catches up to me. "I'll go to the games room. You go to the library."

On my way, I peek under the piano outside the dining room. Then I notice the dining room door is open. Harvey's always nosing around that door, desperate to get into the one place that is off limits to him.

I forget about the games room and look inside only to see Chef Miguel marching toward me. Harvey hangs limp in his arms. "Does this belong to you?"

"He snuck away," I say. "I'm really sorry."

Chef Miguel purses his lips and passes Harvey over to me. "The last thing I need is Appleby finding a dog in here." He shakes his head and mutters something under his breath.

"Sorry again," I say and race-walk out of the dining room as fast as I can. Harvey wriggles, happy to be in my arms. He has no idea how close he came to getting himself kicked out of Brayside.

Maggie's on her hands and knees looking under furniture in the library when I show up. "Look who I found," I whisper.

She heaves a sigh of relief. "Where was he?"

"Dining room."

Maggie's eyes go wide. "No!"

I nod and kind of smirk because it's a little funny when you think about it.

"Harvey! You are so naughty!" Maggie clips Harvey's leash to his collar before I put him down.

"We're lucky Ms. Appleby didn't find him," I say.

"She'd have banned him for life."

I leave the library first and give Maggie the all-clear, so she knows it's safe to follow. We arrive at the Kowalski's suite as the residents are trickling out.

"We never consulted Charlie about our social events. Why should we let Ms. Appleby know?" Mrs. Fradette says to Artie. "You know what I always say, better to ask forgiveness than permission!"

"I never heard anything," Artie says. He draws a finger across his lips, makes a turning motion at the corner, and tosses the invisible key away.

"I'll book the band right away," says Mr. Singh.

Mrs. O'Brien and Miss Lin are discussing baking and Mr. Santos is explaining to Artie how the room should be set up.

Listening to all of them make plans and work together reminds me of how it used to be around here. Maybe when Ms. Appleby sees how much fun it can be at Brayside, she'll relax a little and things can go back to normal.

Chapter 24

Harvey

At dinnertime on Tuesday, Harvey assumes his usual spot on the floor between Maggie's little sisters. He can count on at least one of them to drop something for him. His attention is mainly focused on falling food, but he can hear Maggie's voice go up and down with frustration.

"Ndidi still doesn't have her lines memorized for the first scene! I had to feed them to her and I didn't even need to look at the script. Honestly, Mom! It's so unfair. It's like she's not even trying." There's a pause, and then Maggie speaks again. "I think she has a boyfriend. I heard her tell someone she couldn't come to rehearsal because she had to go to *Koby's* hockey game." Maggie's foot taps with irritation under the table. "She only got the part because she's in eighth grade."

Harvey is rewarded for his patience when a piece of meat slides off a fork and lands on the floor. He gobbles it up quickly, then sits back to wait for more.

After dinner, Harvey is resting comfortably, just about to drift off, when he hears one of his favorite words. *Walk.*

Instantly alert, he runs to the back door to see if it's true. Indeed! Maggie is holding his leash and his plaid coat. He stands still while she attaches the Velcro around his middle. He's gotten a little rounder through the winter and the coat is snug.

As soon as the door opens, Harvey takes off at a quick trot to the sidewalk. The neighborhood is his domain, and there is always work to be done.

They don't make it far before Harvey needs to stop. Gordie has been here recently. He's marked a tree, so Harvey does the same. *Hello, friend*, his squirt says.

There's a commotion up ahead. Rosie, the Westie from a few doors down, has spotted him and is dragging her owner closer. Harvey does the same. All twelve pounds of him go into high gear and there's nothing Maggie can do but give in and run with him. The two Westies meet nose to nose then circle each other, wagging their tails and tangling the leashes.

When Maggie's phone rings, Harvey pays it no mind. The sound is familiar and he'd rather focus on new smells. "Hang on, Harvs," Maggie says, juggling the leash, her phone, and the tricky business of removing her glove.

Harvey knows the voice on the other end of the FaceTime call. Although after months of not seeing the person it belongs to, it has become a distant memory. If he could smell Lexi, it would all come flooding back, but a voice? This is not of consequence to a ratter like Harvey.

As soon as Maggie has herself sorted, Harvey trots ahead, eager to ensure that everything is in order in his neighborhood. "What's up?" Maggie asks.

Lexi gives an exaggerated sigh. "Ndidi! She's not serious about her role! She's barely learned any lines! The musical is starting sooner than she thinks. I also heard her say that it's not a priority."

Maggie's footsteps slow. Harvey strains at his leash. "She said that?"

"Yes!"

"Then why did she take the role? If it wasn't a priority, she shouldn't have taken the lead."

"That's what I said!" There's another familiar voice. It belongs to Brianne.

Maggie has now come to a full stop. Up ahead, Harvey spots a squirrel race down a tree and across the sidewalk. He takes off after it, almost yanking the leash out of Maggie's hands.

Maggie reins him in as the girls keep talking. "You need to tell Mrs. Alvarez that you should be Annie! I saw you at rehearsal today. You know all the lines. You're practically already off-book. Ndidi's going to ruin the musical. You're the understudy. You have to say something."

The squirrel is headed for an oak tree and by the time Harvey arrives, it's escaped up the trunk. *Outwitted again!* From the branches, the squirrel chatters, taunting him. Harvey waits at the bottom of the tree, hoping the squirrel will reappear.

"So, are you going to do it? Let Mrs. Alvarez know you're ready to step up?"

"Mrs. Alvarez gave Ndidi the role for a reason." Maggie's voice is tense. She tugs on the leash, pulling Harvey away from the tree and back to the sidewalk.

"Yeah, she felt bad for her because of her mom."

"What are you talking about?" Maggie strides ahead, and Harvey runs to catch up. He likes to go first; it's in his nature.

"Her mom's got cancer or something."

Maggie's steps falter. "I didn't know about her mom." A gust of wind smacks Harvey in the face, blowing back his beard. "I better go," Maggie says. "My fingers are freezing." Truth be told, now that they're facing the wind, Harvey's paws are also feeling the cold.

"Call me later. Let me know what you decide to do," Lexi says.

"Bye, Harvey! Bye, Mags!" Brianne sing-songs.

Maggie lets out a long sigh. It's so heavy with dismay that it draws Harvey's attention away from his favorite fire hydrant. When Maggie's eyes meet his, he knows, in that way that dogs do, that his Maggie needs him. He scampers ahead of her, ready for whatever is coming their way.

Chapter 25

Austin

I stand inside the front doors of Brayside, stamping my feet trying to get feeling back in them. My flimsy running shoes are no protection against the cold.

"Hey, Austin!" Louise says. She's with Mrs. Gelman, who is shuffling down the hallway with her walker. It's been decorated with red ribbons for Valentine's Day. "Guess who else is here," she says.

As soon as I hear the jangle of keys coming from the hallway, I know the answer.

"Hey, Grandpa," I say, grinning.

"Isaac had a few questions," he says. "And I thought since

I was here, I'd hang around and check in with everyone. The place looks great. Isaac is doing a good job. You are too, from the sounds of things."

"Thanks, Grandpa. I wish Ms. Appleby thought so." Her new rule banning me from doing simple repairs still stings. Grandpa didn't think it made sense either, but since he's not the custodian at Brayside, there wasn't much he could do.

"She'll come around. She's just settling in. Wants to make sure everyone knows who's boss." He greets Mrs. Gelman and then she and Louise continue to the games room, leaving Grandpa and me alone in the hallway.

"Did you see Mr. K?" I ask.

"Not yet. Peeked in on Mrs. Gustafson and Mrs. O'Brien." Grandpa rubs his belly, so I guess he got the double chocolate chunk cookies she'd been saving. "Louise filled me in. Alice is still in the ICU."

I nod. "Mr. K hasn't left his room much." He says it's because he doesn't want to miss a call from the hospital, but I think it's more than that. After being married for over sixty years, he doesn't know how to be without her.

As we walk down the hall, I notice Grandpa eyeing the baseboards. They get scuffed up from the scooters, walkers, and canes. "Don't worry. I did touch-ups last week," I tell him. He's a stickler for details, which is why Brayside is in such good condition. It's also why he got promoted.

I knock on Mr. K's door. "It's Austin. Are you there? I've got a special visitor!"

It takes Mr. K a minute to get to the door. It's only been a few days since I saw him, but he looks like he's aged ten years.

"Phillip!" Mr. K says when he sees Grandpa. His mouth curves into a smile, but it doesn't reach his eyes.

"How are you, Bob?" The way Grandpa asks I can tell he's looking for the truth, not just "Fine."

"I've been better," Mr. K says. "Worried about Alice."

"Up for a visit?" Grandpa asks. "I'd love a cup of coffee. Smells like you just brewed a fresh pot."

I'm a little surprised when Mr. K nods. "A visit would be nice." I guess Harvey's not the only one who can work magic on the residents.

There's music playing in the suite and when I look around, I spot where it's coming from. "That's cool," I say. "I always thought this was just a cabinet."

"You've never seen a hi-fi before?" Grandpa asks.

I shake my head and go over to take a closer look. It's a big, wooden piece of furniture. The top has been opened and underneath is a turntable. A record is spinning below the needle and the music is coming out of speakers below.

"Talking with Austin got me thinking about the dances

during the war. Made me nostalgic, I guess. I pulled out some of the old records Alice and I used to listen to."

As Mr. K pours the cups of coffee, I flip through the stack sitting beside the record player looking at the names: the Jimmy Dorsey Band, the Andrews Sisters, and Frank Sinatra.

"Who're we listening to now?" Grandpa asks.

"Glenn Miller, one of my favorites."

It's not like any music I've heard before. There's the *rat-a-tat-tat* of drums, some horns, and the beat kind of swells. Then someone starts singing in a smooth voice.

"This is the kind of music you were telling me about," I say, "that the bands played at dances."

Mr. K nods. "I was telling Austin about the summer of '42, when I met Alice."

"Middle of the war. You must have been just a kid."

Mr. K crosses his arms, leans back in his chair, and takes a deep breath. "I grew up a lot that summer."

"Because of the telegrams?" I ask.

"Yeah, there was that. Other stuff too. It all started with Freddy Wainwright." The way Mr. K settles into his kitchen chair, I can tell we're in for a story.

Chapter 26

Maggie

Just like every day for the past week, Maggie has lunchtime rehearsals. The whole school is a flurry of activity as the day of the opening draws nearer. The math department has agreed to help with props, and tickets for all performances are being sold at a table in the front hallway. Other girls are preparing costumes with the home ec teacher. Annie's red short-sleeve dress is already hanging on a rack in the theater. The special locket Annie wears is there too, looped around the hanger. A cruel reminder to Maggie of what she *won't* be wearing come showtime.

Before they go their separate ways, Maggie tells Sooyeon about last night's conversation with Lexi and Brianne. "If it's true that Ndidi's mom is sick, I feel bad for being hard on her," Maggie says. "No wonder she can't make it to all the rehearsals." Her forehead creases with guilt.

"Maybe Ndidi doesn't want people to know. She might like her privacy," Sooyeon says, except she says *privacy* with a British accent, which makes Maggie smile.

When she gets to the theater, Maggie spots Ndidi off to the side running lines. Maggie wonders if Ndidi's aloofness comes from having a boyfriend, or from being one of the popular girls in eighth grade. Or maybe…something else?

"Want help?" Maggie asks, sitting down.

"That'd be great," Ndidi says. "I don't know why I'm having such a hard time remembering lines."

"Maybe you have other things on your mind."

Immediately, a shadow crosses Ndidi's face. "I'm not letting anything get in the way of this part, if that's what you're thinking." Her tone defensive.

That isn't what Lexi had said on the phone last night, but Maggie doesn't argue. "I didn't mean—"

Ndidi narrows her eyes at Maggie. There's a chill to her voice. "Start at the beginning of Act Three," she says curtly.

Maggie puts her energy and focus into the script. She doesn't just run the lines, she puts emotion into them, as if she were on-stage. A few girls nearby, including Lexi and Brianne, turn to listen.

"You're really good," Ndidi concedes when they finish

the scene. "A lot better than Koby, and he's usually the one who helps me." Koby is the hockey-playing boyfriend Maggie has heard her mention. Ndidi has missed a few rehearsals because of his games.

"No problem," Maggie says. It's nice to know her hard work hasn't gone completely unnoticed. It's just too bad the compliment came from Ndidi and not Mrs. Alvarez. As she goes to sit with the other seventh graders on a riser behind Ndidi, her phone buzzes with a text. It's from Lexi.

You're so much better than Ndidi. TALK TO MRS. A!

The bossy tone of the text is typical Lexi and sets Maggie on edge. She wonders if Lexi is really worried about the musical or is just trying to stir up trouble. Talking to Mrs. Alvarez about Ndidi could backfire. What if Mrs. Alvarez gets mad at her for sticking her nose where it doesn't belong?

Lexi is the last person Maggie wants to take orders from. But she also doesn't feel like explaining all that in a text, so she sends back a thumbs-up emoji and hopes Lexi will drop it.

Chapter 27

Austin

"Who was Freddy Wainwright?" I ask.

Mr. K leans back in his chair. "There was a gang of us, all about the same age. Me, my best friend Vernon, Carl, and Freddy. Freddy was the unofficial leader and the one with the imagination. With the flying school open and pilots coming from all over, Freddy got it in his head that we'd be a prime target for Nazi spies."

"Nazi spies?" I raise my eyebrows, incredulous.

Mr. K gives a lopsided smile. "You know how kids are. We wanted to be part of the action. Vernon was the artistic one and he made us RAF patches to wear. We flashed them to each other like a secret handshake. We used to meet up behind an old shed to plan our Nazi-hunting strategy.

"'Let's make a list of everyone we suspect of being a Nazi,' Freddy said. Of course, we listed off the people we didn't like. Our teacher that year was top of the list. We added a couple others, like Vernon's neighbor, but only because he'd yelled at Vernon's dog for digging up his garden. 'There has to be more,' Freddy said. 'Come on, fellas, think!'

"Larry Davidson had started hanging around with us that summer. He was one of Alice's cousins and a little younger than the rest of us. All he wanted to do was impress Freddy. 'I got one!' he said. 'My cousin's dad is German!'

"'Which cousin?' Freddy asked.

"A cold lump formed in my stomach when Larry said, 'Alice, the one staying with us. Her last name's Schmidt.'

I wouldn't admit it to the boys, but after seeing her at the dance and peering out the window at me when I'd delivered the telegram, I had a bit of a soft spot for her and didn't take kindly to Larry's accusation.

"Freddy looked at us, gleeful. 'Kinda coincidental, donchathink? Her showing up the same summer the flying school is open?' He raised his eyebrows.

"'You think the Nazis sent a girl to spy?' I asked.

"'It'd make sense,' Vernon said. 'Who'd suspect her?'

"'Has she done anything suspicious?' I asked Larry.

"He thought for a minute. 'She was writing a letter yesterday. Said it was to her mother.'

"Freddy snorted. 'Ha! Her mother! Of course she'd say that. It's probably to her commander—in code!'

"Vernon and Carl nodded, impressed at Freddy's ability to see through Alice's trickery. 'So what do you want to do? Report her to the constable?'

"Freddy shook his head. 'Nah, we don't have enough proof yet. We're gonna watch her for a while. Wait for her to slip up. In the meantime, we need to come up with a plan.'

"'A plan for what?' I asked.

"'Revenge!' Freddy fired back. 'We can't sit back and do nothing, not with a Nazi spy in our town!'

"I hated the Nazis as much as the next person, but I still wasn't convinced that Alice was one. And then, a part of me worried Freddy was right. What if she was involved in a Nazi plot to spy on the flying school? I didn't want to be responsible for letting a Nazi slip through my fingers."

The phone in Grandpa's pocket rings. He stands up to dig it out of his pocket and checks the caller ID. "It's your mom," he says, and answers. "Yeah, he's here," Grandpa says, looking at me. He listens for another minute, then hangs up. "We gotta go," he says. "Something's wrong with Bertie."

Chapter 28

Austin

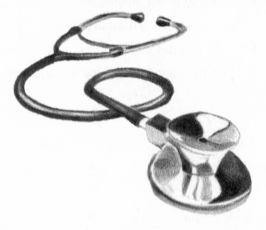

When Grandpa and I arrive at the apartment, there's no yip of greeting or scurry of feet to the door.

"Mom?" I call.

"In here," she says. We go to my room. Bertie's on her lap, wrapped in a blanket, just lying there. Her tail gives a weak wag, and then she looks up at me with her chocolate-brown eyes. She looks like someone just told her the saddest story in the world.

"What happened?" I ask, sinking down to the floor. Mom strokes Bertie's back and talks in a low voice.

"She found this. It must have been under your bed

or something." Mom holds up a small plastic army soldier. Grandpa and I used to play with them when I was little. Most of it has been chewed up so there's just a mangled bit of legs left.

"Oh, no." I look at Bertie. Eating my homework is one thing, but plastic is another.

"I called Dr. Gunn at the shelter. She said to bring her in right away. Plastic is sharp and it could puncture her stomach."

Vets aren't cheap and I don't know if we can afford to go. But looking at Bertie, I don't know how we can afford not to.

I hold Bertie on my lap all the way to the animal shelter. It's the same place I took her after Harvey and I found her abandoned in the alley. Back then she was so small she fit in my hands. She's bigger now, but still fragile. Still in danger. Mom parks and carefully helps me out of the car, so we don't jostle Bertie. Mom's words about the sharp plastic ring in my head.

Bertie's quiet. Normally she'd be squirming for freedom, excited to explore a new place. She is definitely *not* herself, and I'm worried that what she ate might have done real damage.

Mom goes to the desk and checks in, showing what's left of the army guy to Dr. Gunn. I stroke Bertie's head and run my fingers over her floppy ears. "I'm sorry I didn't keep you safe," I say.

Mom warned me not to leave things lying around. I knew the army guy was wedged between my nightstand and the wall, but I was too lazy to pick it up. If I'd listened, Bertie wouldn't be wrapped in a blanket on my lap, waiting to see the vet. I hold her a little tighter and try to stop myself from thinking about worst-case scenarios.

For the last half an hour, Bertie's barely moved, but all of a sudden she lurches forward, and I grab her to keep her from falling. *Is she trying to jump down? Does she want to go outside?* Her stomach heaves, and she opens her mouth, gagging. "Mom!" I call, panicking. *What's happening to my dog?*

Bertie's body shakes. She gasps like she's choking and can't get enough air. I don't know what to do. "Mom!" Bertie makes that noise again. "What's wrong with her?"

Mom runs over. Her eyes are wide and worried.

Bertie gags again, but this time something comes out. A glob of grossness lands on my shoe.

I stare down at the puppy puke and see a hunk of mangled plastic. Mom spots it too. "Good girl, Bertie!" she says.

Dr. Gunn comes over. I cringe watching her pick up what's left of the toy. I mean, she's wearing Latex gloves, but still. It's disgusting. "Is that all of it?" she asks.

Mom compares what's in her hand to what came out of Bertie. "I think so."

I hold Bertie as Mom mops up my shoe. "That's a good sign," Dr. Gunn says. "I'd still like to examine her, just to be on the safe side."

Dr. Gunn leads us to a room and points to a metal table.

"You can put her there," she says. "Gently."

I unwrap the blanket. Bertie looks up at me and I give her a reassuring smile. "It's okay," I say, hoping that's the truth.

Dr. Gunn puts her stethoscope against Bertie's belly and listens for a moment. Then, she prods her in certain spots. Bertie doesn't flinch. Dr. Gunn flicks her ponytail over her shoulder and glances at me. "I remember when Bertie came in. You found her, right? In an alley?"

I nod. "Actually, it was my friend's dog who found her."

Dr. Gunn smiles. "The same friend that surprised you?" I nod, remembering the first time I held Bertie and knew she was mine. Dr. Gunn's brown eyes are kind when she looks at me. "I think you're in the all-clear. Keep an eye on her and only feed her little bits of soft food and water. If you see blood in anything— her water dish, her poop, or urine—bring her in right away."

"So, you think she's okay?" I ask, hardly believing it.

Dr. Gunn puts the stethoscope around her neck. "I think she's a lucky little dog, Austin. For lots of reasons."

The bill for the vet wasn't as bad as it could have been. But I still saw Mom's mouth tightening as she used her credit card— the one that's only for emergencies.

"Austin," Mom says as we're walking to the car. The way she says my name, I think I'm in for a lecture about keeping my room clean. "I promise I wasn't snooping, but I found this when I was sitting with Bertie." She pulls out the Edu-Trek form from her purse. It's the one where I've already filled in my name and written that I want Amar to be my roommate. The only thing missing is the box marked Deposit or Pay in Full. "I thought you didn't want to go on this trip."

It's what I told Mom when the e-mail to parents first went out. We'd just got Bertie and I knew we couldn't afford it. Back then, I didn't know the whole class would be going.

"If you want to go, we can figure something out. I'm sure I could find a serving job somewhere. With tips—"

I shake my head. That would have helped a few months ago, but the deposit is due at the end of next week. "It's okay, Mom."

"Do you want me to talk to Mrs. Becker? Explain the situation?"

It's what my heart wants, but I know it'd be asking for too much. Besides, today was a close call. What if something else happens to Bertie? I'd hate to think I spent the money she might need. "No. I just wrote that stuff on the form to make Amar happy. I don't want to go. Honest."

I hold Bertie a little closer and ignore the way my stomach twists at the lie.

Chapter 29

Maggie

On Friday, Ndidi is absent for *another* after-school rehearsal. There are grumbles from a few of the girls. Even Mrs. Alvarez seems unnerved by it.

"I've practiced more with Maggie than with Ndidi," mutters Priya. She's been cast as Daddy Warbucks.

Maggie's holding a prop from the previous scene: a beat-up suitcase Annie takes as she leaves the orphanage. She squeezes the suitcase handle, hoping Mrs. Alvarez will realize that taking a risk on Ndidi isn't worth it. That she'll officially move Maggie into the lead role.

"I think we'll end a little early today," Mrs. Alvarez says after

Maggie and Priya finish their scene. "You've all worked hard this week." There's a round of applause from the girls, and a few sighs of relief. "Maggie," Mrs. Alvarez calls. "Can I speak with you?"

Maggie's careful not to get her hopes up. She was fooled once before. But still...she can't help wondering if this is it. The moment Mrs. Alvarez asks her to replace Ndidi. .

"Ndidi's missed a lot of rehearsals this week," Ms. Alvarez begins.

And the week before, Maggie silently adds.

"You're doing a great job learning the lines and the blocking."

Maggie glows at the compliment and readies herself from what she's sure Mrs. Alvarez will say next.

"So, I was thinking, it'd be great if you got together with Ndidi on the weekend and went over things. Get her up to speed."

Maggie swallows, trying to hide her frustration.

"Normally, I wouldn't ask, but Ndidi needs a little extra support."

Maggie doesn't want to be unsympathetic, even though a little voice in her head screams *It's not fair!* But what can she do? She gives Mrs. Alvarez a quick nod.

Her teacher looks relieved. "Thanks, Maggie. I knew I could count on you."

Maggie is too irritated to text Ndidi right away. If Ndidi can't commit to the musical, then she shouldn't be in it. Maybe she should do what Lexi suggested and tell Mrs. Alvarez that she's going to drop out unless she is allowed to replace Ndidi.

But ultimatums aren't Maggie's style. She doesn't want to leave the musical. Even though all her free time has been dedicated to rehearsals this month, she likes it. Being part of a big production is fun.

Maggie decides that if her teacher is willing to give Ndidi another chance, then she should be too. She texts Ndidi offering to meet. Ndidi responds, but it turns out she lives as far from Maggie's end of town as possible, and probably can't get a ride to Maggie's house.

Maggie isn't ready to give up.

We could meet somewhere in the middle. Somewhere on a bus route.

That's when Maggie gets a great idea. There is one place that has the space for them to practice, is centrally located, and is available.

Do you know where Brayside Retirement Villa is?

Chapter 30

Harvey

Smells bounce off brick buildings and metal dumpsters in the alley behind Brayside. It is a jumble of scents, and for a moment Harvey stands still, his nose quivering, trying to capture them all.

Maggie presses the buzzer. Harvey's keen ears hear it ring inside, over the hum of the car's engine and Maggie's anxious throat-clearing. It is an unusual way to enter Brayside, but Harvey has no reason to worry. He is with his Maggie, and there is no danger—at least not in the alley.

When the back door opens, Maggie scoops Harvey up before he has a chance to greet Austin properly. "Any Appleby sightings?" she asks as she waves good-bye to her dad and slips inside.

"Not yet."

The door opens into a small room with empty boxes, some discarded furniture and a nurse's cart with a broken wheel. Beyond all this is another door, one that opens to the main corridor. Austin slinks along the wall and peeks around the corner. Maggie follows, still carrying Harvey. Like two spies with a secret package, they make their way past Mr. Singh's suite, then Mrs. Gelman's, and stop at the Kowalskis'. The man with the slippers. A sadness has come over him lately. Harvey senses it in the same way he can smell lingering odors that have long since become undetectable to the human nose.

He also knows, without Maggie telling him, that he is meant to comfort this man. He has a job to do here. Just before they go into Mr. Kowalski's room, Maggie puts her lips close to Harvey's ear. "I'm going to meet a friend. You stay with Austin and Mr. Kowalski." She gives Harvey an extra squeeze: a nudge of encouragement and gratitude for what she knows he will do.

Chapter 31

Austin

Coming to Brayside today was a good distraction from other stuff. Namely, Mom's job hunt. She's been extra stressed since she found the Edu-Trek form, and I wish I was a better liar. She totally knows I want to go on the trip and has doubled her hunt for a job.

Mr. K pulls out a chair at the kitchen table, but Harvey has other ideas. There's no spot for him there. He sits by the couch, tilting his head at us like, "Aren't you going to join me?" He even whimpers once. Mr. K sighs and gives a little laugh. "Guess Harvey's the boss." As soon as Mr. K gets settled, Harvey jumps up and lies right next to him.

I get a little catch in my throat because that's what he used to do with Mr. Pickering too, another resident I used to visit. We sit quietly for a few minutes, but it's not awkward or anything. The clock ticks the minutes by. Harvey's already asleep, lulled by Mr. K's closeness.

"I was telling you about Freddy and the boys last time, wasn't I?"

I nod. "Yeah, you thought Mrs. K was a Nazi spy."

"That's right," he says with a snort-laugh. "The evidence against Alice grew at each meeting. Just like Freddy had asked, her cousin Larry had been keeping an eye on her and this one day, he showed up with a bombshell. He'd overheard her on the phone, speaking German!

"'Who was she talking to?' Vernon asked.

"'She *said* it was Uncle Heinrich,' Larry answered, but the way he said it sounded like he had his suspicions.

"'She could be lying,' Carl said. 'A Nazi spy would do that.'

"'Or, it *could've* been her dad,' I muttered, not wanting to believe Alice would work for the Nazis.

"'Anything else?' Freddy asked Larry.

"'Well,' he paused. 'I know I was supposed to be watching her, but she tricked me.'

"'What do you mean?' Freddy asked.

"'Larry hung his head. 'We were playing hide and seek, but I don't think she ever really hid. I looked all over and couldn't find her.'

"'Exactly what a spy would do!' Freddy said. 'She might've been meeting up with her commander.'

"'You think she's got a commander?' Carl asked.

"'Someone recruited her. It could've been her dad. He's German, ain't he?'

"'Being German doesn't make her a Nazi,' I reminded them.

"'Yeah, yeah. But look at all the evidence we got,' Freddy said.

"I had to admit it wasn't looking good for Alice. 'Do you think she went to the flying school when Larry couldn't find her?' I asked.

"'There's always people watching the planes,' Freddy went on. 'No one would care about a girl walking between the buildings. She could even say she's delivering something and then—'

"'Sneak inside!' Carl finished.

"My stomach sank. I'd read enough Johnny Canuck comics to know there'd be top-secret information at the flying school. Aerial photographs of enemy territory, plans for missions, and who knew what else?

"That's when an idea came to me. 'You know, fellas,' I said. 'If we're gonna catch a spy, we gotta think like a spy.'

"'What do you mean?' Vernon asked.

"'Well, we need to get close to her without her suspecting anything.'

"'Uh-huh. That's why we got Larry.'

"Now, no offense to Larry, but I wasn't sure how dedicated he was to his job. I'd seen him at the movies one afternoon, and Alice was nowhere around. Another time, he'd been playing tag with some boys at the airfield. 'Nazis are sneaky, you said so yourself. So we gotta be sneakier.'

"A sly smile spread across Freddy's face. 'What are you thinking?'

"I ran down the list of things we knew about Alice and ended with her being a good dancer. 'That's the ticket right there. Once a girl has a dance partner, they might spend all evening together.'

"Vernon's eyes opened wide. 'Who wants to do *that*? It's not just dancing with a Nazi, you gotta dance with a girl!'"

Mr. K pauses to chuckle. "I was a little more advanced than Vernon. Dancing with a girl, especially one who looked like Alice, sounded okay to me!"

I interrupt Mr. K. "But you said you didn't know how to dance."

"That's right. I didn't, but if I wanted to find out the truth about Alice, I was going to have to learn. I swallowed my pride and asked my mom for help. I'm telling you, Austin, I'd have died if any of my friends caught me. She was pleased as punch, though. Every night after dinner Mom tuned into a program called *Here Comes the Band* on the radio. We'd practice to each song that came on."

I bite back the cringey face I want to make. Dancing with Mom would be right up on my list of things I never want to do.

Harvey hasn't moved a muscle while Mr. K's been talking, but a knock at the door startles him awake. When I get up to answer it, he jumps down from the couch and trots over to join me.

Mrs. Fradette and Mr. Singh are standing in the hallway. Mrs. Fradette's eyes are always magnified by her glasses, but they get bigger when she sees Harvey.

"*Crab*appleby is here," Mrs. Fradette whispers.

"She must have found out that some of us were enjoying ourselves and has come to put an end to it," Mr. Singh says.

I look at Mr. K sitting on the couch. I hate to cut the story short, but I have to warn Maggie. "I'll be right back," I say and glance down at Harvey. "Don't you leave this room," I tell him in my sternest voice. He plants his butt on the floor and looks up at me, blinking like I have nothing to worry about.

I'm halfway to the library when an unfamiliar man walks in. He's carrying a satchel, the kind you use for work and flashes an official-looking badge at the receptionist. "I'm here to see Hilary Appleby," he says.

The way he surveys the foyer puts me on edge.

"Hey, Artie," I say and grab him as he comes out of Mrs. Gelman's suite with his nursing cart. "Who's that?" I nod in the man's direction.

Artie tries to cover his surprise with a cough. "The health and safety inspector." He shoots me a look. "That explains why Ms. Appleby's here. She didn't want to miss his visit."

On one hand, I'm relieved that Ms. Appleby doesn't have some kind of sixth sense about Harvey—she always seems to show up when he's visiting—but on the other hand, what's going to happen if this inspector finds a non-certified comfort dog who isn't following any of Ms. Appleby's protocols? I can tell by Artie's face he's thinking the same thing.

"I'll warn Maggie," I say. I keep my eye on the inspector as I phone her. She doesn't answer, so I send her a text. *Code Red!* That means, get Harvey and get out of here. I'm about to race down the hall to where she's practicing but before I can, Ms. Appleby appears. She's got her clipboard. "I've made some changes around here," she says to the inspector. "I think you'll be pleased."

Chapter 32

Maggie

Maggie and Ndidi work for an hour in the library, pausing often so Maggie can show Ndidi a note she's made on blocking in her dog-eared script. Despite missing so many rehearsals, Ndidi picks up on the blocking quickly and has memorized most of the first act. Before starting Act Two, they decide to take a break. "How do you like St. Ambrose?" Ndidi asks. The girls are sitting on top of the tables, their legs dangling over the edge. Maggie packed snacks and hands a granola bar to Ndidi.

Maggie shrugs. "I like it."

"You're friends with Lexi, right?" Ndidi asks.

Maggie treads carefully. "We went to the same elementary school and were good friends then."

Ndidi reads between the lines. "But not now?"

"We're into different things," Maggie answers tactfully.

"She texted me a while ago and told me you were after my part," Ndidi says. "And that I should watch my back."

Maggie almost chokes on her food. "What?"

"That's why I was sort of worried about working with you when Mrs. Alvarez suggested it. I thought you might try to sabotage me or something."

Maggie's eyes flare open. "I would never do that!"

Ndidi gives her an apologetic look. "I know," she says quickly.

"Why would Lexi lie?" She, Lexi, and Brianne used to be best friends. They did everything together, equal in all ways. But now their relationship is like an unbalanced teeter-totter. Lexi keeps finding ways to make it clear that she has the upper hand.

"She probably feels threatened because you're more talented," Ndidi says.

Maggie doubts that's the reason. "Mrs. Alvarez doesn't think so. She gave Lexi the better role." Maggie sighs. "You know what's sad? None of Lexi's backstabbing surprises me anymore. Since we started at St. Ambrose, she's become a different person."

"Yeah, I know what you mean," Ndidi says, shaking her

head. "Everyone acted all happy that I got the lead, but then behind my back, they say I got the role because Mrs. Alvarez felt bad for me."

Maggie doesn't want to pry, but she's curious about how much of what Lexi told her is true. "I heard your mom is sick."

"She had breast cancer three years ago, and now it's back."

All the confused feelings Maggie had for Ndidi are washed away in a flood of sympathy. "Oh. I'm sorry, Ndidi. That's terrible."

Ndidi's gaze drifts to the floor. "The chemo makes her really sick. My dad's doing the best he can, but he's gotta work. I'm trying to help out, make sure my little brother gets to hockey and stuff, but it means I have to miss rehearsal."

At the word *hockey* Maggie realizes she had Ndidi pegged all wrong. "Is Koby your brother?"

"Yeah."

Maggie gives a rueful shake of her head. "I thought he was your boyfriend. And you weren't at rehearsal because you were watching him play hockey."

Ndidi lets out a loud giggle. "My boyfriend!"

Maggie feels silly now, but she's glad to see Ndidi laughing. "I couldn't believe Mrs. Alvarez was letting you off the hook so easily." Now Maggie is laughing too.

"Let's make a deal," Ndidi says. "We have each other's backs, no matter what. Those other girls, they can—"

"Stick it in their ear!" Maggie finishes, channeling her

inner Mrs. Fradette. Ndidi holds out her hand. Maggie takes it, and they shake. Maggie makes another deal, a silent one with herself. *I will no longer listen to anything Lexi has to say.*

Chapter 33

Harvey

Harvey sits at the door waiting for Austin to return. He doesn't mean to disobey, but when the nurse's aide arrives, she props the door open to wheel in her cart. For a curious dog like Harvey, the open door is an invitation to find out where Austin has gone.

The boy's scent is fresh and easily discovered. But the farther Harvey trots from Mr. Kowalski's suite, the more tangled the scents become. He keeps his nose on the ground, careful not to miss any. It is only as he zigs and zags down the hall that he catches a whiff of a smell that jogs his memory. The mysterious trail from the other day!

With renewed determination, Harvey sets off to find the source.

He raises his head once and spies Austin talking with Artie, but they are deep in conversation and don't notice him. Like any good investigator with a suspect in his sights, he stays focused. Once again, the smell leads him to the dining room. The doors are open and Harvey seizes his chance to race inside.

Chapter 34

Austin

From the corner of my eye, I see something streak past and turn the corner into the dining room. "Was that—"

"Harvey!" Artie gasps.

Ms. Appleby and the health and safety inspector are at the nurses' station, and their backs are to us. It's pure luck they didn't see Harvey.

I glance at Mr. K's suite, but the door is closed. For a second I wonder if my eyes are playing tricks on me, but then the door opens, and out comes the nurse's aide with her cart. "Oh no," I groan. He escaped—again!

"I'll stall the health and safety inspector," Artie says. "Get Harvey out of there!"

"And take him where?" I ask. Artie shrugs.

"Hi there," Artie says loudly. He holds out his hand to the health and safety inspector and angles him away from the dining room entrance. "I'm Artie Mendoza."

I don't hang around to listen. I pass the library where Maggie and her friend are rehearsing. There's no time to stop and fill them in. Instead, I race-walk to the dining room.

I can't believe that, of all places, Harvey would come here! It's the one place he can *never* go. We've broken a few, okay, *all*, of Ms. Appleby's rules by bringing Harvey to Brayside today. I don't want to think about what will happen if he's found.

One of the dining-room doors is open. I walk through and shut it after me so Harvey can't escape. Miguel is belting out a Spanish love song. If he has his earbuds in, he won't be able to hear anything.

"Harvey!" I call. "Harvey, come here. I have a treat." I'm lying, but desperate times call for desperate measures.

The dining room is big. There's lots of tables and chairs and a buffet set up along one wall. I don't see Harvey anywhere, and I'm starting to panic. *Where is he?*

That's when I hear a yip. It's the excited bark that tells me, he's found something and wants someone to know. It's coming from the kitchen. I run across the room. One of the swinging doors is propped open. Miguel whisks something in a bowl, unaware that Harvey has snuck in. He turns to me in surprise when I burst into his kitchen.

"Austin!"

Harvey is frozen in place, head low over his paws. His eyes are like lasers, and his tail is pointed straight back. "He's got something," I say. I take a few steps closer, and Harvey doesn't budge. He's completely focused on what he's found. I peer over Harvey's head and see that he has managed to corner something furry, gray, and about the size of a golf ball.

A mouse!

I wave Miguel back because if we scare the mouse, Harvey will take off after it. I've seen how he chases squirrels. He'll tear through Brayside trying to catch it.

"Is that a—?" Miguel can't even say the word. Mice might be common in some places, but not in a high-end retirement home like Brayside and definitely *not* in the kitchen.

"What are we going to do?" he asks.

"Chef Miguel!" It's Ms. Appleby.

"What now?" he whispers, panicked.

"The health and safety inspector is here," I say.

He says a few things under his breath in Spanish that I'm pretty sure I can't repeat.

The whole time we've been talking, Harvey hasn't moved a muscle. Neither has the mouse. It's scrunched up as small as it can get against the wall. There's nowhere for it to go.

"Chef Miguel!" Ms. Appleby calls again.

"You need to stall them. Don't let them come in here until you see me leave," I tell him.

"How am I supposed to do that?"

The bigger question is, how am I supposed to get a mouse and a dog out of the kitchen without anyone noticing?

Chapter 35

Maggie

S omething's not right. Maggie can sense it. Through the side-lights on either side of the door to the library, she can see lots of movement. She's supposed to be focused on the scene with Ndidi, but instead, her attention keeps drifting. "Hang on a sec," she says, putting her script down. "I need to see what's going on."

Maggie opens the door to find Mrs. Fradette, Mr. Singh, and Mr. Kowalski scanning the hallway and peering around corners. "Oh! Maggie," Mrs. Fradette says loudly. "I didn't know you were here! Look, Vikram! Maggie! And a friend!"

Ndidi grins at them, but Maggie is instantly suspicious. "What are you doing?"

"Nothing," Mrs. Fradette and Mr. Singh say at the same time.

"We lost Harvey," Mr. Kowalski replies, matter-of-factly. The other two hang their heads.

"Where's Austin?" Maggie frowns. "He promised he'd look after Harvey."

All three of the old people look at each other with a new worry. "Warning you that Crabappleby is here!"

"Who's Crabappleby?" Ndidi asks.

"She means, Ms. Appleby, the new assistant director," Maggie explains. She does a quick job of introducing everyone. "Ndidi's in the musical," she says, choosing her words carefully. There's no time to admit she lied, and Ndidi was the one actually cast as Annie.

Artie appears, looking flustered. He mops his brow with a hankie.

"Harvey got out again," Maggie says to him.

"I know, but that's not the worst part. Mr. Chang, the health and safety inspector, is here. I stalled him and Appleby for as long as I could, but then Mr. Santos needed help. Did Austin get Harvey?" he asks.

The old people shake their heads.

Artie's face pales. "Uh-oh. Then, we have a problem. Harvey went into the dining room."

Maggie quickly puts things together. "If Ms. Appleby and the inspector find Harvey before Austin can get him out of there…" Her voice trails off.

All of them rush to the dining room with Mr. Singh leading the charge on his scooter. Ndidi shoots Maggie a gleeful look. "This isn't what I thought a seniors' home would be like," she whispers.

"It's not always like *this*," Maggie says. She's a little breathless because she, along with Austin and Artie, blatantly broke a rule, and they will all get in trouble. Not such a big deal for her and Austin, but this is Artie's job. She would feel terrible if he got fired.

Mrs. Fradette moves beside Maggie and grabs her hand. "Play along, dear," she says. "Yoohoo! Ms. Appleby!" she calls and barges into the dining room, with Maggie in tow.

The rest of them aren't sure what to do, except follow.

Chapter 36

Harvey

Harvey's entire body is tensed. Every muscle on high alert now that the creature has been cornered. It is small, but its scent is strong. As a ratter, Harvey's job is to chase creatures like this one and catch them if he can. His instincts make it impossible to back away.

Harvey keeps his eyes trained on the mouse. He can hear noise in the background. There are familiar voices. Austin is nearby, but Harvey blocks everything out. His attention is on the mouse.

A new scent momentarily distracts him. It is one of Harvey's favorites. Peanut butter! From the corner of his eye, he sees Austin rest a wooden spoon at the top of a bucket, like a ramp. It is a testament to Harvey's dedication as a ratter that he doesn't investigate either the smell, or what Austin has made.

"Easy, Harvey," Austin says and gently grasps Harvey's collar. Austin has a dollop of peanut butter on his finger too, and waves it in front of Harvey's nose. The temptation is too much for this Westie. His focus is broken as he licks the deliciousness off Austin's finger.

The mouse sees his chance. It too, can smell the peanut butter. Boxed in by a wall, a cabinet, and Harvey, its only choice is to run up the wooden spoon and get the peanut butter reward.

Just like Austin planned, as soon as the mouse gets to the top of the spoon, it tips into the pail and the mouse falls in. "Yes!" he says, with a fist pump. "Problem number one, solved!"

Harvey's treat is abruptly taken away as Austin goes about covering the pail with a rag. He picks Harvey up and takes the pail by the handle. Harvey doesn't like feeling helpless when there is a job to do. He squirms, but Austin fixes him with a stern look. "Stop, Harvey." It is his 'I-mean-business' voice, so Harvey obeys.

From up under Austin's arm, Harvey gets a look at the kitchen. The counters are filled with supplies and shiny metal tools. But Harvey is attuned to smells and, from his vantage point, he knows that this is not the only mouse at Brayside. Where there is one mouse, there are many.

If only Austin would let him down, he could show him.

Chapter 37

Austin

The mouse is safe in the bucket. The sides are too high and too slippery for it to climb out, but I put a lid on it anyway. Harvey's still squirming like he's got more work to do in here. And on the other side of the kitchen door, we can hear voices. Mrs. Fradette is speaking loudly to Ms. Appleby, probably to warn me about what I already know—we're in deep doo-doo!

"Margaret wants to be a health and safety inspector, don't you, dear?" I hear Mrs. Fradette saying in the dining room. Her voice is getting closer. "What a coincidence that she's here the same day as you!"

Maggie launches into a story about being at a restaurant and finding a millipede in her dinner. "It was disgusting! Imagine if I'd eaten it! I'd have a millipede family living in my digestive system!" That gets everyone else sharing what disgusting things they've found in restaurant food.

I've got to get the mouse, Harvey, and myself out of here. Chef Miguel is thinking the same thing. He's forgotten about the pot simmering on the stove and has his hands pressed to either side of his head, as if he can squeeze the answer out of his brain.

I open one of the kitchen's swinging doors a crack and peek out. The inspector is getting impatient and is trying to escape the conversation. Maggie is at the back of the group, looking worried. She spots me. I point at the dining room door and duck back into the kitchen. With one shoulder against the door, I wait.

"I love the kitchen!" Maggie says. "It's always such a surprise to see what Chef Miguel is cooking."

"I don't usually have this many people joining me on inspections," Mr. Chang says, irritated.

"I have an idea, let's all close our eyes and try to guess what's cooking in there right now. No peeking! You too, Mr. Chang," Maggie says. I've never heard her so sound so perky.

"Great idea!" someone else says. It's a young voice, so it must belong to Maggie's friend. She takes a big breath. "Something tomatoe-y and—is that peanut butter?"

I push the door open. Maggie has her hands up around the inspector's face like blinders. Mrs. Fradette motions for me to make my move, as Maggie says, "Keep those eyes closed. It will help you focus all your energy on your sense of smell."

"I really don't have time for this," Mr. Chang says. He barges into the kitchen at the same moment I leave it. Ms. Appleby and the inspector are now in the kitchen and don't notice me race through the dining room with Harvey under my arm and a mouse in a bucket.

Chapter 38

Maggie

"**C**an we rehearse here again?" Ndidi asks. Everyone has made their way back to the Kowalskis' suite, leaving Ms. Appleby and Mr. Chang to continue touring Brayside. "This is the most fun I've had in a long time."

Maggie's glad Ndidi enjoyed herself. After a few hours at Brayside, she looks less stressed than she did when she arrived.

A fresh pot of coffee is brewing when there's a knock at the door and everyone freezes. "It feels like we're under house arrest," Mrs. Fradette grumbles. But it's just Artie.

"The coast is clear," he says. "Mr. Chang left and Ms. Appleby is in her office. She'll get his report next week."

Harvey trots over to say hello and Artie looks around the room. "Where's the mouse?"

The empty bucket sits in the corner of the room. "I did what Grandpa would have done," Austin says. Maggie doesn't want to know what that means exactly, but she agrees with everyone that mice at Brayside spell disaster. "Isaac better call the exterminators ASAP, or Appleby will have to hire Harvey as a full-time mouse catcher." Maggie and Austin share a look because that's actually a really good idea.

"Harvey saved the day!" declares Mr. Singh.

"And how about Margaret? What a performance!" Mrs. Fradette says with a wink in Maggie's direction.

"I totally believed that you wanted to be a health and safety inspector," Ndidi says.

"You'll have a good story to tell Mrs. K when you visit her tomorrow," Maggie says.

Mr. Kowalski makes a noise in his throat. A funny look comes over his face.

"What is it, Bob?" Mrs. Fradette asks.

"Alice's condition has changed to critical." Mr. K's voice is gruff. "She's on a ventilator now."

Mrs. Fradette goes over and puts her hand on his. "Oh, Bob. I'm sorry. Your poor Alice."

All Mr. K can do is nod. He's pressing his lips together but his chin trembles. "I never thought I'd have to be without her. Seeing her in the ICU with that machine…she's so fragile."

"She's not fragile, Bob," Mrs. Fradette says. "She's fighting, and you have to give her a reason to. Remind her of all the things worth coming back for. Her children and those grand-kids! And you, of course."

"Don't forget Mrs. O'Brien's blueberry muffins," Austin says. That makes Mr. Kowalski smile.

"The Valentine's Dance," Maggie adds.

"And she can't miss the musical! We have to see our Margaret perform! Our own Annie!"

Everyone keeps offering suggestions to Mr. Kowalski, but Maggie has stopped listening, cursing her tattle-tale cheeks, which have flared from pink to red. Ndidi's eyebrows are pulled together in confusion. Maggie's shame deepens. She never should have lied. *Ndidi probably thinks Lexi is right and I am out for her part.*

Maggie swallows her pride and does what she should have done in the beginning. "Actually, I'm not Annie. Ndidi is. I'm the understudy." She blurts everything out in one breath, hoping that admitting the truth will be easier if she does it quickly. "I didn't tell you because I didn't want to disappoint you." She can't bear to look at anyone's face—especially Mrs. Fradette's.

"Margaret," Mrs. Fradette says and takes Maggie's hand in hers. "You could never disappoint us."

Maggie is surprised at the surge of emotion she gets hearing Mrs. Fradette's words. To her relief, Ndidi doesn't look angry.

"Understudy sounds important," Mr. Singh says.

"It is. She has to learn *all* the roles, not just mine. It's a big responsibility," Ndidi says. Even though their friendship is only at its beginning stages, Maggie can tell Ndidi is someone she can trust.

"It's too bad though. With your hair—"

Mrs. Fradette clears her throat and cuts Mr. Singh off. Maggie feels so much better now that the truth is out in the open. She wonders why telling it felt so impossible before. She should have known the old people would understand and she feels foolish for thinking they wouldn't.

Chapter 39

Austin

I've been training Bertie to sit and wait while I clip the leash to her collar. Today is the first time she does it. She also let me sleep in until seven o'clock this morning and hasn't had an accident inside in a few days. While she's still calm, I run my hand from her neck to her tail. *My puppy is growing up.*

Outside, Bertie's little legs move quick to keep up with me. Harvey always walks with purpose, like he's got to be on the lookout. Bertie's more happy-go-lucky and all over the place, bounding on her little puppy legs from one spot to another.

She stops to sniff at a corner, but as soon as I tug her leash, she leaps back into action, scampering along beside me. I look down at her, and she looks at me. When our eyes meet, I can tell what she's thinking: *I'll follow you anywhere.* Even though it's cold outside and I forgot my hat, I feel warm all over.

Grandpa decides to join me at Brayside. Yesterday's "mouse-ca-pade" got him worried. When the sliding doors whoosh open and Grandpa enters, he's greeted like a local celebrity. Mary Rose shoos everyone back to work and looks up at Grandpa. "I'm glad you're here because I'm not sure how much more of this I can take," she says through a clenched jaw. "Miss You-Know-Who gave me a binder—a binder, Phillip!—of new protocols I'm supposed to follow."

"You're the head nurse," Grandpa says. "She can't do that."

"Exactly," Mary Rose says. "I've asked Charlie about a transfer to Walker Terraces when it opens."

My jaw drops. Brayside can't lose Grandpa *and* Mary Rose. "But, Mary Rose—" I start.

She shushes me with a look. "It's not just all these new rules. I told her about the money that went missing from the locked drawer and guess what she did?" Mary Rose doesn't wait for us to answer. "She decided to install a security camera over the nurses' station! I won't work in a place where I'm not trusted. Not after so many years."

I don't blame Mary Rose for being upset, and I wish there was something I could do. I've run through all the possible scenarios to explain the money's disappearance, but nothing makes sense. Isaac doesn't have a key and wouldn't take his own money. Louise has a key, but she's worked here almost as long as Mary Rose and wouldn't risk her job for two hundred dollars. Artie doesn't have a key—or at least, that's what he told me. I guess he could have been lying. But Artie? Miss Lin cleaned him out in three games of poker. That guy can't lie to save his life.

The last person who has access to the drawer is Mary Rose. Sure, I've heard her talk about money being tight, but would she really steal? From Isaac?

Mary Rose leans in close to Grandpa and says, "If I go, Louise and Artie aren't far behind."

With all her safety measures, Ms. Appleby is single-handedly ruining Brayside.

Mary Rose rounds on me. "Although thanks to *someone*, Artie almost didn't have any choice in the matter."

I silently groan. By the look on her face, Mary Rose heard what happened yesterday with Harvey.

Grandpa gives a low chuckle. "Better go check in with Isaac," he says, abandoning me. Before he walks away, he mouths "Good luck." Getting on the wrong side of Mary Rose is never a good idea.

"A dog in the kitchen! My word! I'm not joking about Artie losing his job! And who knows about Chef Miguel!"

"I know," I say hanging my head. "It was a total accident."

Mary Rose sighs. "You know I love that little dog, but if you and Maggie can't watch him properly, he can't visit. Not with Appleby cracking down on us about every little thing."

I stare at Mary Rose. She was the one who encouraged me to keep Harvey when I found him. "It won't happen again," I promise. "And anyway, if Harvey hadn't gone in the kitchen, we never would have known about the mouse problem."

Mary Rose's eyebrow arches higher, like she's daring me to keep talking. I decide to quit while I'm ahead.

"I think I'll go see Mr. Kowalski," I say changing the subject.

I thought Mary Rose would be happy that I want to visit with him, but instead, her face falls. "Before you do…"

"What?" I ask, my voice catching. "Did something happen?"

Mary Rose frowns. "He's not well, Austin. The trips back and forth to the hospital are hard on him. He's not sleeping properly, and his appetite has really dropped off."

"Did he go to the hospital to see her today?"

Mary Rose shakes her head. "He said he didn't feel up to it."

"Not up to it?" I mutter to myself. It sounds like he's the one giving up, not his wife.

Mr. K answers the door wearing his housecoat and pajamas. From the hallway, I can see the plate of food that was delivered for breakfast, but he hasn't touched it.

"Grandpa's meeting with Isaac," I explain. "I wondered if I could wait in here until they're done."

Mr. K nods and shuffles back inside. He sits down heavily at the kitchen table.

"Want me to make some coffee?" I ask.

"That'd be nice," he says. I've watched him do it before and try my best to get the measurements right. By the looks of him, he wouldn't notice if I put coffee or green slime in his mug.

"How about some music?" Listening to that record the other day lifted his spirits. Maybe it will work again.

But this time, Mr. K shrugs like he doesn't care one way or the other.

I go to the hi-fi and find a record with a band on the cover. The Jimmy Dorsey Orchestra. *It's worth a try.* I slip the record out of the sleeve and put it on the turntable. with a flick of the power switch, the record starts spinning. When I drop the needle, there's a moment of static and—

The horns start. And the drums. I mean, wow! This kind of music gets your attention. At the kitchen table, Mr. K turns my way. He blinks a couple of times like he's just noticed I'm there. "That's the Jimmy Dorsey Orchestra," he says.

The coffeemaker beeps. When I put the mug in front of Mr. K, he reaches for it right away, takes a sip, and smacks his lips. "Not bad, Austin." I don't know if Mr. K wants to talk, or just sip his coffee and listen to music. Either one is fine with me.

The coffee in my cup vibrates a little. When I look over, I see Mr. K's foot is tapping under the table. "You could tell me more about being a telegram delivery boy," I say.

Mr. K takes a long sip of his coffee, considering, and then starts talking.

"There was a hopeless feeling that hung in the air that summer. The adults felt it more than the kids, but there was no escaping it. With so many of our boys away, it was only a matter of time until real tragedy hit Neepawa. I think I told you how Mr. Erstwhile warned me when a telegram was bad news. 'You might want to get a neighbor for this one,' he'd say and point out the Commonwealth seal and the address on the front. I appreciated the heads-up.

"It was halfway through August when he got sick and a new man took over. Mr. Slezak didn't know the town well, and, unlike Mr. Erstwhile, he didn't put the telegrams in order. He'd just hand me the stack and send me on my way. I'll never forget the day I delivered one to Mrs. Graham. She handled it as well as can be expected, considering she'd just lost her son. But since Mr. Slezak hadn't organized the telegrams, I was almost finished deliveries when I discovered a second. Turned out she'd lost both of her sons." Mr. K breaks off and lets out a heavy breath.

"The pride I felt at having a job and doing something to help the war effort had started to pale. None of the reports from overseas were good. The mood in town had changed.

People worried when they saw me cycle up their sidewalk, and rightfully so. More often than not, I was bringing bad news. It weighed on me, this job. But whenever I thought about quitting, I remembered my brother, and all the other boys fighting overseas, and I kept at it. But trust me, watching Vernon, Carl, and Freddy enjoying their summer was a thorn in my side. They kept up their meetings, determined to catch a Nazi. I begged off, more often than not, feeling too grown up for their games.

"It was about two weeks after Slezak started that I pulled the last telegram out of my bag. It was a white envelope with a purple Commonwealth seal. More bad news most likely, I thought to myself, and checked the address. Time stood still when I saw whose it was…. Mine."

"What'd you do?" My voice is almost a whisper.

"I stuffed the telegram back in the bag. I wanted to pretend it didn't exist. I thought about ripping the telegram to bits. Burning it, or tossing it in the river. If it never got delivered, than the news, whatever it was, wouldn't be real. But, of course, I couldn't do that. It wasn't fair to Andrew, or my mom. She deserved to know what had happened to him.

"I don't know how I did it, but I got back on my bike and rode home. My feet were as heavy as lead when I walked in the house. The radio was on and Mom opened her mouth to scold me about wearing my shoes inside. Then she saw my face. Her eyes went to the envelope I was holding. Her whole body stiffened.

"'Give it here,' she said, and held out her hand. Mom ripped the envelope open and pulled out the telegram. Her hands trembled as she read the message. I braced myself, sure that Andrew had been killed, knowing I was now the man of the house.

"She gasped and slapped her hand over her mouth, shaking her head as if she couldn't believe what she'd read. I waited for her to wail, or cry. I prayed she wouldn't faint. I didn't want to be alone waiting for her to come to.

"'Bobby.'" Her voice was a hoarse whisper. 'He's alive!'

"I grabbed the telegram from her hands, not believing it. *Private First Class Andrew Kowalski...wounded...recuperate...Kingston, ON....receive honorable discharge.*

"The smile that lit up Mom's face," Mr. K pauses and shakes his head, "it was a miracle, it really was.

"A song came on the radio right then. "Chattanooga Choo Choo" by the Jimmy Dorsey Orchestra. Mom grabbed my hands and started dancing with me right in the middle of the kitchen. The steps were all wrong, but we didn't care. She flung me around the kitchen, and together we whooped and hollered that Andrew was alive.

"'My boy's coming home!' she said, laughing and crying at the same time. Neither of us talked about what injuries Andrew might have, or how bad they might be. All that mattered was that he was alive. The war hadn't taken everything."

Mr. K looks away, lost in the memory. "There's not too many times I felt joy like that. It taught me that no matter how bad things might seem, there's always hope, always a chance, they'll get better." Mr. K's voice catches. When he looks at me, his eyes are watery. "I need some of that hope right now, Austin."

Chapter 40

Maggie

On Monday, Maggie fills Sooyeon in on the excitement at Brayside. Between Harvey's escape, the mouse hunt, and their ruse with the health and safety inspector, Sooyeon is belly laughing as Maggie finishes the story.

"Something must be funny," Lexi says, sidling up to Maggie and ignoring Soo. Her skirt is rolled rebelliously high. The laugh dies in Maggie's throat. "Did you talk to Mrs. Alvarez about that *thing* we discussed?" Lexi points her chin in a silent signal.

Talking with Ndidi has opened Maggie's eyes to a few things, mainly that she can't trust Lexi. "No, and I'm not going to."

"Why not?"

Maggie's frustration boils over. "It's none of your business, and you know what else?" With as much Mrs. Fradette spunk as she can muster, she says, "You can take your advice and stick it in your ear, Lexi." Maggie slams her locker shut and together, she and Sooyeon walk away.

Lunchtime rehearsal is going well. Lexi isn't there because none of her scenes are being rehearsed. Maggie sits off to the side mouthing the words along with Ndidi, who is on stage. Their weekend practice paid off.

Rehearsal is in full swing when the school secretary appears and asks to speak with Ndidi. The conversation is short, and a moment later, Ndidi hurriedly collects her things. A few girls roll their eyes. One mutters something about commitment under her breath. Maggie is glad Lexi isn't here.

"I'll go with you," Maggie says, jumping up from her seat.

Ndidi shakes her head. "You have to stay. Mrs. Alvarez needs an Annie." Her hands tremble and the script slips to the floor. She's more rattled than she's letting on.

Maggie shakes her head, adamant. *Mrs. Alvarez might need an Annie, but you need a friend.*

As soon as they're in the hallway, Ndidi takes a deep, shaky breath.

"Is it your mom?" Maggie asks.

Ndidi nods. "She's at the hospital. Dad's picking up Koby

and me." They head to the front doors to wait for Mr. Udo to arrive. "You'll have to fill in for me after school too," Ndidi says.

"That's fine," Maggie says.

Ndidi sighs. "Mrs. Alvarez should just give you the role."

Maggie shakes her head. "You're Annie," she says firmly. "Opening night is still a few weeks away."

"Mom will be done her treatments by then," she says. "We'll be through the worst part."

Ndidi's dad pulls up outside. "Thanks, Maggie," she says and leans over and gives Maggie a hug. "You're a good friend."

Maggie's cheeks flush at Ndidi's words. She plays them over in her head for the rest of the afternoon. When it's time for after-school rehearsal, she sets her jaw, daring anyone to make a negative comment about Ndidi.

Chapter 41

Austin

"What's up with you?" Amar asks at lunch.

I have to come clean with him, I don't have the money for Edu-Trek. No one's hired me for babysitting or dog walking, and my offer to do custodial work at school got a hard no from Ms. Khokhar, our principal.

"It's Edu-Trek," I start. "I don't know if I can go." Amar nods like he's not surprised. *Maybe this won't be as hard as I thought.*

"I had a feeling this was coming."

"You did?"

"Yeah, the way you were talking, I figured there was

more going on. You don't need to worry though. I've got it
all sorted out."

"You do?"

"Yep! I talked to my mom and she said it's no problem."

"Wow!" I laugh, part with shock and part with joy. "That's
so nice of her. I'll pay her back, I promise!"

Amar waves my offer away. "Nah, don't bother. She's happy
to dogsit for free."

My breath catches in my throat. "Dogsit," I repeat.

"I could tell leaving Bertie was the problem, so I asked,
and she said she'd be happy to watch her. Your mom can pick
her up after work each day. Problem solved." Amar slaps his
hands together like it's a done deal.

I gulp. "That's awesome," I mumble. "Thanks."

Amar launches into all the cool things we'll do on the trip
and shows me another promo video for the water park we'll go
to in Quebec. I fake smile my way through it. My insides are
screaming at me to tell him the truth, but I can't. The lie has
become too big.

I think about faking an illness just before the trip.
Something really contagious, like the bubonic plague.
Is that still a thing? Or I could develop a phobia about planes.
Or maybe, hopefully, there'll be a freak weather occurrence
and the whole trip will be canceled.

After lunch, Mrs. Becker bustles into the class and tells
everyone to listen up for an exciting announcement. I'm

too stressed to pay attention. All I hear is something about a contest and Reggie Diggs.

"Can you imagine?" Amar asks. "Meeting Reggie Diggs in person?"

I give him a half-hearted smile. A baseball player is the last thing on my mind.

When school is over, I want to go home and hang out with Bertie, but I promised Mr. K I'd come by. Brayside is on the way home anyway, so I decide I'll go for a quick visit. Fifteen minutes won't make a difference to me or Bertie, but it will mean a lot to Mr. K.

There's no one sitting in the foyer, which isn't a surprise. Since Ms. Appleby started, the residents stay out of her way. The nurses' station is empty too, but the shiny new surveillance camera has been installed. It points directly at the desk. When I get to the games room, Mrs. O'Brien has her foot up on the coffee table and Louise is holding an ice pack on it.

"What happened?"

Mrs. Fradette, Mr. Singh, and Mr. Santos look concerned. Mrs. O'Brien's cheeks aren't rosy like usual. "I twisted it climbing down from the step stool."

"She was hanging the decorations," Mrs. Fradette explains. Red and pink streamers and sparkly hearts are on the walls.

"You need to stay off it for a few days," Louise says. "It's swollen and you don't want to make it worse."

"Not with the dance just around the corner," adds Mr. Singh.

"What's going on in here?" a voice asks from the door. It's Ms. Appleby and she's got her clipboard with her.

"Oh, just a little mishap. Nothing some TLC can't fix." Louise pats Mrs. O'Brien's arm and stands up.

"You'll have to write a report," Ms. Appleby says, "and send it to me before the end of the day."

"A report?" A bit of attitude leaks into Louise's voice. She puts her hand on her hip. "We don't write reports about things like this."

Ms. Appleby holds her chin up and looks down her nose at Louise. "You do now. Her family will need to be notified."

Louise side-eyes Ms. Appleby. She's got more to say but keeps it bottled up till Ms. Appleby leaves. Then, she mutters. "I've been nursing since that one was in diapers. She thinks she's gonna tell me how to do my job?" She clamps a hand over her mouth. "Oh, Lord. I shouldn't have said that out loud."

"We were all thinking it," Mrs. Fradette says. "She didn't even ask Gloria how she was doing!" Mrs. Fradette throws a sympathetic look at Mrs. O'Brien.

"She hasn't checked on Bob either. Alice has been in the hospital for almost three weeks, and Ms. Appleby hasn't gone by his suite once! I doubt she even knows our names." Mrs. O'Brien sits back with a huff.

Now that they mention it, I've seen Ms. Appleby speak to the nurses, the aides and Isaac, but never the residents— not unless they ask her a direct question. Maybe Ms. Appleby doesn't like old people. And if that's true, then why'd she take the job?

Chapter 42

Austin

I leave the games room and head over to Mr. K's suite. It takes him a few minutes to get the door.

"How's it going?" I ask. I don't ask about Mrs. K because I know there's been no change in her condition.

"I can't figure that thing out," he says and points to the washing machine. "You know how to work it? Alice always does the laundry. All those knobs and dials…"

"Want me to show you?"

"That'd be nice, Austin." Mr. K sounds so grateful, I think he might cry. It's a quick lesson, and the machine starts humming. For once, I'm glad Mom makes me do my own laundry.

I join Mr. K at the kitchen table. But sitting in silence isn't good for either of us, so I get up and go the hi-fi. I look through the pile of records and pull one out. As soon as it starts playing, Mr. K begins to hum.

"I remember this one. 'Frenesi' by Artie Shaw."

"Does it help to talk about back when you first met Alice?" I ask softly, wishing I knew the right thing to say or do.

He gets lost in his memory for a moment, the way old people sometimes do. "I think I told you, I wasn't a regular attendee at Freddy's meetings."

I nod. "You'd kind of outgrown them."

"Between Andrew's injury—we'd found out he'd lost his leg—and delivering telegrams, I knew the war wasn't a game. I'd seen firsthand the pain it caused in a way none of them had.

"It was one of the rare times I attended a meeting that I found out Alice had been ducking out on Larry. He had no new intel, and he was getting frustrated. 'We need to try something different.' Larry turned to me. 'How's your dancing?'

"Now the truth of it was, my regular dance lessons with Mom were a bright spot. I was no Fred Astaire, but I'd gotten better.

"'Good enough to catch a spy?' Freddy asked.

"I shrugged. Larry slapped my shoulder. 'You're goin' undercover, Bob!'

"Freddy laid out the plan. 'Asking her to dance will give you time alone with her. Get her talking and find out what you can. We need all the evidence we can get.'

"I didn't know what I was supposed to talk to her about, or what kind of evidence she might give me, but I was willing to go along with it. It wasn't such a hardship to dance with a girl like Alice. And you know, I was curious. If she really was a spy, how'd she keep it a secret from the rest of Larry's family?

"The next day, I went to my fishing spot on the river-bank. I did all my best thinking there. I was so lost in thought, I didn't hear anyone coming until it was too late. There was a noise in the bushes, and then Alice stumbled out, picking leaves from her hair and swatting at flies.

"My mouth fell open. No one else knew about this place. How had she found it? I thought for a second that she'd followed me.

"'Sorry. I didn't know anyone was here,' she mumbled and turned to go. I was no expert on girls, but it was obvious she was upset. Maybe this was my chance to talk with her. Without a roomful of people and a loud band playing, we could have a real conversation. It was time I knew the truth. Did we have a Nazi in our midst, or not?

"'You don't have to go,' I said, shuffling over to make room for her.

"She paused, looking between the twisty, bug-infested forest path and the peaceful stretch of riverbank. I needed to come up with something to convince her to stay and blurted the first thing that came to mind. 'Wanna fish?'

"She looked at me like I was soft in the head. I held up the extra rod to show her I meant it.

"'I don't know how,' she said.

"'Nothing to it,' I answered. 'Come on, I'll teach you.' My heart skipped with nerves when she took a few steps closer. I had to keep my wits about me—for lots of reasons.

"She squinted at the river, sparkling in the late afternoon sun. 'Guess I better learn now, before I have to leave.'

"'You're going home?' Larry hadn't mentioned that.

"She huffed angrily. 'No, not home. My parents are moving us to Toronto! I leave on Sunday.'

"'Why?' I asked.

"'The war,' she said. 'People in Winnipeg won't shop at a store owned by a German.' She shook her head. 'My dad was born here! He tried to enlist but got turned down on account of his diabetes. He's as Canadian as they are, but all they see is our last name. Schmidt.'

"'But you speak German,' I blurted.

"Alice gave me an odd look. I realized my mistake and quickly added, 'Don't you? I mean, on account of your dad being German?'

"'I know a few words,' she admitted. 'It comes in handy when I don't want Larry eavesdropping on my phone calls. He sticks to me like a flea on a dog.' She flopped down beside me and stared out across the river. 'I hate this war.'

"It was the first time anyone had said that out loud to me.

Mom always kept a brave face, talking about how courageous the boys fighting overseas were. True, our hardships were nothing compared to what the soldiers endured, but hearing Alice say it made me realize I hated the war too. It almost took my brother and it had definitely taken my innocence.

"'Me too,' I admitted. And that's when I told her about Andrew and delivering telegrams.

"She said how much she missed her home. 'It's nice of my aunt and uncle to let me stay, but I've had about enough of my cousins.' I bit back a laugh as she told me the lengths she went to in order to escape Larry.

"We talked so much that afternoon, we scared away the fish. I didn't care. I might have gone home empty-handed, but my heart was full.

"The next day, I called a meeting behind the shed and told the fellas what I'd learned. 'She's not working for the Nazis,' I said.

"Freddy sneered. 'Oh yeah? What was she doing by the river? No fishing pole. No swimsuit or towel. She was probably planning to meet her commander.'

"'I think she just wanted to be alone.'

"'Bah,' Freddy shook his head. 'Come on, Bob! You fell for that?'

"I glared hard at Freddy. 'She's no Nazi!'

"'Larry's her cousin and he thinks she is. Don't you?' He turned to Larry.

"'Larry doesn't know squat,' I fired back. 'Just because

she's half German doesn't make her a Nazi.' I looked at Vernon. He was my best friend, and I thought he'd back me up.

"But he shook his head. 'What's got into you, Bob?' he asked.

"'Nazi lover,' Freddy whispered.

"A deathly silence fell over us.

"I couldn't believe Freddy would say that to me. My brother had lost his leg fighting the Nazis. I'd spent the summer delivering telegrams to worried mothers and wives, and he called *me* a Nazi lover!" Mr. K blows out an exasperated puff of air.

"Part of me wanted to shove Freddy into the shed and teach him a lesson. But I saw the looks on the other boys' faces. They were thinking the same thing he was. 'Don't you ever call me that again,' I said and spat at Freddy's feet. 'I'm no Nazi lover, and you know it. I'm telling you, Alice isn't a spy for the Nazis, or anyone else.'

"I left the boys and didn't look back. I hoped they'd let it go, but in my gut, I knew they couldn't. They'd spent all summer building a case against Alice. It was at the next dance that I found out just how far they were willing to go."

The washing machine buzzer rings. I get up and quickly throw the laundry into the dryer. I glance at the clock. As much as I want to hear what happened next, I don't want Mr. K to wear himself out. He needs to be strong for Mrs. K. But then I think about how he's been alone all day missing his wife and how his face lights up when he talks about the past. *Maybe remembering things is good for him*, I think.

So I slide back into my seat and nod for Mr. K to continue.

"I avoided the boys for the next couple of days. There was a dance scheduled for Saturday, and with Alice leaving on Sunday, it was my last chance to see her.

"I'd never put so much care into getting ready as I did that day. Slicked my hair back with Brylcreem and shined up my church shoes. Mom whistled when I came downstairs. 'Don't you look handsome,' she said.

"It was nice of Mom to say, but there was only one person whose opinion mattered to me."

"Mrs. K's," I say softly.

Mr. K nods. "When I got to the dance, she was sitting with a group of girls from town. The band was playing a song I knew, but as much as I wanted to ask her to dance, going up to a table of girls was too intimidating. What if she said no? Or laughed at me for asking? Then, I saw Freddy and the fellas walk in. Freddy looked smug and the way he set his eyes squarely on Alice put me on edge. *What is he up to?* I wondered.

"Larry came by and I grabbed hold of his shirt. 'What's going on?' I asked.

"'We're gonna get the spy!' he said.

"I held Larry's shirt tighter. 'What are you going to do?'

"Larry leaned away from me, a little wary now. He jerked

himself out of my grip, but I continued. 'She's your cousin, isn't she? You're gonna let them hurt her?'

"'They're not gonna hurt her,' he said. 'Just teach her a lesson. Make sure she knows Nazis can't come to Neepawa.'

"'She's not a Nazi!' I said through gritted teeth.

"'How can you be sure?' he asked. 'Nazis are sneaky.'

"By then, Freddy had moved in front of Alice's table. I did a double take on his outfit—short pants, a tucked-in short-sleeve shirt, suspenders—and realized he was meant to look like a Hitler Youth. Freddy pulled a tin of shoe polish out of his pocket and drew on a small Hitler mustache. All at once, the boy was transformed. He raised his hands and blew a whistle to signal the other boys into action.

"From their spots around the dance hall they goose-stepped, that is marched like the Nazis did, right up to Alice. Then they raised their arms in the Nazi salute, looked at Alice, and said in unison, 'Heil, Frauline Schmidt.'

"Dancing stopped. The room fell silent. My heart hammered. I looked away from the boys, still as statues, arms raised in salute. Alice's face had gone ashen. The other girls at her table leaned away from her, eyes wide.

"If people hadn't known she was a Canadian of German descent, they did then.

"Carl handed Freddy a bowl. It was filled with dirt. He put it in front of Alice and said, 'Eat dirt, Nazi!'

"If it had been me, I would have fled the room in tears.

But not Alice. She stood up, didn't say a word, and glared at the boys.

"It was Freddy who flinched first. If I wasn't already in love with her, seeing Alice stare down Freddy made it official.

"I cleared my throat and stepped forward. 'Alice,' I said, my voice loud in that silent room. 'Will you dance with me?' I held out my hand. Her expression wavered for a second. She probably wondered if this was part of the prank. I looked at her with all the intensity and honesty I could muster. All eyes were on us.

"'I'd be honored,' she said, and walked over to me. She made Freddy look like a fool as she flounced past him.

"I led her to the center of the dance floor and nodded at the emcee. 'How about "Chattanooga Choo Choo"?' I asked.

"He turned to the band and said, 'You heard the man. Let's go, boys,' and the band struck up the song. First time anyone called me a man, and I felt like one right then. I'll tell you, I did." Mr. K's eyes are shining.

"I'll never forget it. Alice and I moved across that floor like a hot knife through butter. We didn't leave each other's side for the rest of the night. When the emcee called out the last dance of the night, Artie Shaw's "Dancing in the Dark," I held Alice's hand tightly. I didn't want the evening to end. "Dancing in the Dark" became our song. We played it at our wedding and every year on our anniversary."

Mr. K stands up and goes to his hi-fi. He lifts the needle,

and from the speakers a song starts playing. It has no words, but it doesn't need any; it's perfect how it is.

Mr. K sits back down, closes his eyes, and hums with the song. For the first time in a long time, he looks peaceful.

Chapter 43

Harvey

Maggie's mom stops the car, and Maggie gets in. "Hi, Harvs!" she says in that high-pitched voice that gets Harvey's tail wagging. "Ready for a surprise trip to Brayside?"

Maggie smells like she always does after a day of school. St. Ambrose is in an old building, and there is a musty smell tinged with fried food from the cafeteria on her clothes. She's been with Sooyeon recently too. Her friend's scent mingles with Maggie's.

Maggie runs her hands down Harvey's back and scratches under his collar. "The best part about going today is that mean Ms. Appleby won't be there. She's on a tour of Walker Terraces."

"Is she's still giving you trouble about Harvey?" Maggie's mom asks. "Even after he saved the day with the mouse?"

"She doesn't know anything about that! Are you kidding? We were breaking so many of her protocols, she'd probably ban Harvey for life."

Harvey trots through the front doors of Brayside like he owns it. He beelines for the dining room and feels a sharp tug on his leash.

"Oh, no you don't!" Maggie says.

But Harvey knows there is more work to be done. The mouse Austin caught wasn't the only one. The scent of others swirls in the air around him.

Harvey looks at Maggie and then in the direction of the dining room. He plants his butt, refusing to move. "You can't go in there," she says.

Maggie's words have little effect on Harvey. On top of being curious and great detectives, Westies are also stubborn.

"Harr-veyy!" Maggie warns, drawing out his name. "Come!"

A noise behind Maggie distracts Harvey. The jangle of keys is familiar, but it isn't Austin's grandpa who appears. It's Isaac, and his hands are full. "Hi, Maggie. Hi, Harvey! I didn't think you'd be here today."

"My mom had some errands to run so she dropped us off. What are you doing?" Maggie asks.

"Ms. Appleby wants all these decorations down. Apparently, it's a fire hazard to have things on the wall. Guess we don't need them now that the dance is cancelled."

"Cancelled?" This is news to Maggie. "Since when?"

"Today. Ms. Appleby doesn't want the residents to get worked up. I guess an event like this would be too much for some of the people with 'conditions'." Isaac frowns. "It's too bad. Miss Lin was working on something special for Mr. Kowalski."

Maggie mutters, "Unbelievable," under her breath. "Have you seen Mrs. Fradette?" she asks Isaac.

"She's in the games room with the others. Hey, if you don't mind, could I borrow Harvey for a bit?"

Harvey hasn't been following the conversation, but his ears perk up at his name.

"The exterminator came and set some traps," Isaac explains, "but he doesn't have Harvey's nose. I want to make sure we didn't miss anything."

Maggie pats Harvey on the head and passes his leash to Isaac. "Be good, Harvs," she says. "I'll see you soon."

Harvey watches his Maggie walk away. The familiar tug of wanting to be with her pulls at him, but then Isaac crouches down and blocks his view. "Harvey, we have a job to do," he says. "The mice are out there. All you have to do is lead me to them. Are you ready? Let's go!"

Harvey has no idea what Isaac has said, but he likes the spirited tone. It only takes him a moment to realize that

Isaac is willing to let him explore. Every inch of Brayside can be sniffed and investigated. Finally, the enemy invader will be discovered.

And defeated.

"What are you doing?" The sharpness of Ms. Appleby's voice sends a jolt through Harvey. She's just walked in from the cold. The breeze from outside stirs the air.

"I thought you were on the tour at Walker Terraces," Isaac says.

"Evidently. It ended. I came back to catch up on some paperwork. You haven't answered my question. Why is the dog with you?"

Just then, Harvey catches sight of something in his peripheral vision. *A mouse!* It darts under a piece of furniture. Harvey races after it so suddenly that the leash flies out of Isaac's hand.

Harvey is well and truly free to chase after the mouse without restraint. His body is built for sprints and tight turns, but he's no match for a mouse running for its life. The mouse leads him past the door to the basement to a corridor he's never been in before. The signs on the doors read Staff Room and Medical Supplies.

In the time it takes Harvey to blink, the mouse disappears, but Harvey refuses to give up. He puts his nose to the floor and doubles back, tracking the scent into another unfamiliar space.

"Why's he going into my office?" Ms. Appleby cries.

Harvey follows the scent across the room to a filing cabinet and presses his nose to the small gap between it and the wall. His reward is a bonanza of odors. Harvey gives a yip of victory and paws the carpet. *Success!*

Behind him, Isaac and Ms. Appleby appear. Isaac clicks on a flashlight. The light illuminates the spot where Harvey is sniffing.

"He did it!" Isaac shouts, triumphant. "Harvey found the nest!"

"The nest?" Ms. Appleby's voice rises an octave. She takes a few steps backwards to the door.

"That's right!" Isaac bends down on all fours and meets Harvey's gaze. He pats Harvey on the head. "Let's go tell Maggie that my number one mouse catcher did it again."

Chapter 44

Maggie

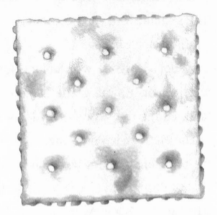

Maggie goes to her room and dials Austin's number as soon as she gets home from Brayside. She has a lot to tell him. "Do you want the good news, or the bad news?" she asks when he answers.

"Good news first."

"Harvey found the mouse nest. Guess where it was?"

"I don't know…the library?"

Maggie waits a beat before answering. "Ms. Appleby's office!"

The irony of the situation is perfect. "She was worried about everyone else breaking rules, and she had an open box of crackers on her desk," Maggie says. "Isaac figures the mice had been feasting on them for a while."

"Okay," Austin says after they've stopped laughing, "now the bad news."

"Appleby called off the Valentine's Dance! She made Isaac take down the decorations and canceled the band." On the other end, Austin is silent. "Did you hear me?"

"I heard you. I just don't believe it."

"What can we do? Everyone was looking forward to it. They secretly elected Mr. Kowalski the Duke of Valentine's Day. Miss Lin showed me the sash she made for him." It's a wide red ribbon, and Miss Lin has embroidered *Duke* in capital letters down the front of it. She worked on it for days. And Mrs. O'Brien's baked dozens of cookies, even though she had to stand on her bad ankle." When Austin says nothing, Maggie continues. "And that's not the worst part." Maggie takes a breath. "Mrs. Fradette is serious about moving to Walker Terraces!"

"Really? She'd move?"

"She said she didn't move into Brayside to be told what to do. She'd rather leave than put up with all Ms. Appleby's rules." While Maggie enjoys spending time with all the residents, it's Mrs. Fradette she cares about the most. "If she goes, the others might follow her."

"Mary Rose said the same thing," Austin admits. "She's fed up too."

Maggie can't bear the thought of all this change. "We have to do something."

She looks down at Harvey, absently combing her fingers through the coarse hair on his belly. As usual, he has made himself comfortable beside her. *Isaac broke a lot of rules letting him sniff out the mice, but it was worth it,* she thinks. *He got the result he wanted. Maybe it's time for all of us to take action.*

"Keeping everyone safe is Ms. Appleby's only concern," Maggie says. "But if she saw the residents actually having fun, maybe she'd realize that's important too."

"What are you saying?" Austin asks, but there's a grin in his voice.

Maggie knows he's thinking the same thing as she is. "The band might be canceled, but the dance doesn't have to be."

Chapter 45

Austin

"Austin?" Mrs. Becker asks. "Do you know the answer?"

I stammer for something to say. I thought we were still in language arts, but yesterday's math homework is what's on the Smartboard. Everyone's eyes are on me.

"No, I don't," I mumble.

"Is your homework done?"

I shake my head. Disappointed, she moves on to the next person.

Amar turns to me with a glad-I'm-not-you expression. I spent last night looking up songs for the Valentine's Dance playlist. I remembered the names of the bands Mr. K had played for me and downloaded a bunch of their music. One song I didn't add was "Dancing in the Dark." It's special to the Kowalskis. I wouldn't feel right playing it unless Mrs. K was there.

The playlist was my job. Maggie and Sooyeon were making new decorations.

"Austin?"

I jump at Mrs. Becker's voice and look around. The lunch bell rang and I didn't notice. Amar ditched me to get to the cafeteria for Pizza Wednesday.

"You've been distracted all morning. What's going on?"

"Uh, well…" I shift in my seat.

"Are you still worried about Edu-Trek?"

The class trip has been on my mind, but it isn't what's *really* bothering me. The deposit is due at the end of the week. Mom had another job interview and she said it went really well. But I've heard that before. Anyhow, even if she gets the job, she wouldn't start for a while. Getting the money together in time is pretty much impossible at this point.

Mrs. Becker's blue eyes soften as she waits for me to spit it out.

"It's about Brayside. One of the residents is in the hospital, and she's not getting better. Her husband, Mr. Kowalski, told me about these dances they went to when they were kids during the war." I pause.

"Go on," Mrs. Becker says.

"I did some research. Music can help people who are sick. I always thought the piano concerts Mrs. Gustafson gave before meals was for entertainment, but it turns out music is good for lots of reasons." I pull up an article I found on my phone last night and read part of it out loud. "Whenever memories have an emotional context to them, they tend to hold much more power in the brain and tend to be processed differently." I give her a meaningful look. "When Mr. K told me about the song they danced to, I wondered if playing it for Mrs. K would help her get better, you know because of the 'emotional context.'"

There's a long silence as Mrs. Becker studies me. "Is this what you've been thinking about when you should have been doing your homework?"

There's no point lying. "Yeah," I whisper quietly. I guess to most people, my idea sounds ridiculous, and kind of hopeless. I'm no doctor. If it had a chance of working, they probably would have tried it by now.

"I'm not sure what to say," Mrs. Becker says, frowning. "I've never had a student like you."

I wish I hadn't said anything, especially when she pushes back her chair and stands up. "Wait here. I'll be back in a minute."

When she returns, I realize I'm in more trouble than I thought. She's brought Ms. Khokhar, our principal with her! "Austin, tell Ms. Khokhar everything you told me."

I gulp. "Everything?"

Mrs. Becker nods. "Don't leave anything out."

Ms. Khokhar adjusts her headscarf as she sits down. I launch into the whole story about how the Kowalskis met and how Mr. K stood up to Freddy and the other boys. I tell them about how much Mr. K misses Mrs. K. "I'm worried that if she doesn't get better, he's going to get sick too. I never understood the saying 'Died of a broken heart' until I got to know Mr. Kowalski. I'm worried that's what might happen. They've been together for so long. I know school is supposed to be my priority, and I shouldn't get distracted, but…it's hard to concentrate when all this other stuff is going on." It feels good to finally say it out loud.

"I can understand how that would be challenging," Ms. Khokhar says. I peek at her. She doesn't sound angry. In fact, both her and Mrs. Becker smile like they want to give me a hug, not a detention.

"You told me about Brayside, but I didn't realize how involved you were with the residents," Mrs. Becker adds.

I sit back in my chair. "You're not mad?"

Mrs. Becker laughs. "Well, you should be paying attention during class," she says, "but we're proud of you. I wanted Ms. Khokhar to hear the story too."

Ms. Khokhar gives me a big grin as she stands up. "Connecting with the elderly is so important. Will you keep me posted on the Kowalskis?"

"Yeah, for sure."

Mrs. Becker and Ms. Khokhar share a look as she leaves. Then Mrs. Becker says, "So back to your idea about playing music for Mrs. Kowalski. What's getting in your way?"

"Well, the main problem is I don't have a way for Mr. K to play the music. I made a playlist, but it's on my phone."

Mrs. Becker stands up. "I think I can fix that. Come with me."

We go to a room attached to the library. It's crammed with props used for musicals, old textbooks, and science lab equipment. Basically, it's where school stuff goes to die. She opens a cupboard labeled Audio Visual and pulls out a machine that looks as old as my mom. It probably is that old, because when the heck was the last time anyone listened to music on a cassette tape?

Mrs. Becker finds a blank tape. "You can use this to record the songs on your phone," she says.

I hold out my hands and take the tape recorder. It's clunky, but if it does the job, I'm not complaining.

I spend the rest of lunch hour in Mrs. Becker's room. I hold my phone right up against the tape player and press the red Record button a few seconds before I start the song on my phone. As soon as the song is finished, I press the Stop button.

The lunch hour is more than half over when I finish. "Thanks, Mrs. Becker," I say. "I can't wait to play this for Mr. K."

Mrs. Becker gives me one of her crinkly-eyed smiles. "You

know, I pass Brayside on my way home. Would you like a lift after school?"

It's another freezing day outside. Her offer is a no-brainer.

"I'll call your mom to get permission. See you at three-thirty," she says. I leave her classroom and grab my lunch. Then head to the cafeteria with "Chattanooga Choo Choo" playing in my head.

Mrs. Becker's car has heated seats, and I wish the trip was longer because my butt is just getting toasty when we pull up to the front doors of Brayside. I thought she was just going to drop me off, but Mrs. Becker parks the car and turns off the engine.

"You're coming in?" I ask.

"After hearing your stories, I'd like to meet the residents."

"They love meeting new people, especially Mr. Singh. Just don't get Mr. Santos started on his stamp collection," I warn her.

There are good smells coming from the dining room, but no crackling fire. The foyer is empty, and I notice some new signs. One on the mantel says, No Fires Permitted. Another one on the wall reads, Keep Walkways Free. And as we head to the games room, I see another. Maximum Capacity 50 People'. I roll my eyes.

Mrs. Fradette and Miss Lin are chatting on the couch in

the games room. Mr. Singh is beside them on his Cobra GT4. "Austin!" they exclaim together.

"You're here a little earlier than usual," Mr. Singh says checking his watch. "And you've brought a guest."

"This is my teacher, Mrs. Becker," I say.

"Miriam," she corrects and shakes their hands.

"I bet Austin is a wonderful student," Miss Lin says.

Mrs. Becker gives me a wink. "He constantly surprises me."

"He's the same here!" Miss Lin answers enthusiastically. "We're so lucky to have him. So helpful." Hearing her kind words makes me blush.

"Is that a tape player?" Mr. Singh asks. I'm holding it in my hands because it was too big to fit in my backpack.

"It's from school. Mrs. Becker let me borrow it. I'm working on something for the Kowalskis." I plug in the tape player and press play.

Ten seconds into the first song, Mrs. Fradette's eyes widen behind her thick glasses. "That's 'Dancing in the Dark!' My parents loved Artie Shaw. I haven't heard it in years."

"It's a special song for the Kowalskis. I thought if Mr. K played it for Mrs. K the next time he's at the hospital, it might help."

Their faces fall. "What happened?" I ask. No one says anything. I get a sinking feeling in my stomach. *Am I too late? Did Mrs. Kowalski—oh, I can't even think it. Please, please let her be okay.* I steel myself for the worst.

"The doctors called this morning," Mrs. Fradette says.

"They told Bob to be prepared to say his good-byes," Miss Lin says gently. She hesitates. "She probably won't make it through the night."

My mouth goes dry and I get a hard lump in my throat. It's going to be the hardest thing I've ever done, but I have to see Mr. K. Now, more than ever, he needs me.

Chapter 46

Maggie

There's no rehearsal scheduled for after school and Maggie is looking forward to leaving at regular dismissal time. She and Sooyeon made plans to work on the decorations for the surprise Valentine's Dance and then order pizza. It's the first time they've been able to hang out in ages.

Maggie walks past the theater on her way out and hears someone singing. Did she make a mistake reading the schedule? Maybe she does have rehearsal!

She peeks inside. Ndidi is alone on stage. She was at school today, the first time since her mom was admitted to the hospital. Through texts, Ndidi has kept Maggie posted on her mom's progress. The chemo drugs are working, so her mom's doctors want to keep her on them. Even if they make her sick, it's better than the alternative.

Maggie nudges the heavy wooden doors open a little more. "From the top," Mrs. Alvarez says. Ndidi opens her mouth and begins to sing "Tomorrow." Free of a soundtrack, or of a chorus of girls behind her, Maggie hears what Ndidi really sounds like, and her jaw drops.

Maggie has a good singing voice. She knows that, but it pales in comparison to Ndidi's. Each word Ndidi sings comes from deep in her gut.

Ndidi reaches the crescendo and takes a breath. When she lets loose, the final chorus gives Maggie goosebumps. Ndidi is singing the song as Annie, but as herself too. She pours emotion into each lyric.

Maggie lets the door shut quietly. Now she understands why Mrs. Alvarez picked Ndidi for the role. It had nothing to do with pity, or being in eighth grade. Ndidi got the part because not only is she talented, but she understands Annie in a way other kids can't. She might not be an orphan, but if anyone can relate to desperately wanting their family back together, it's Ndidi.

Chapter 47

Austin

I'm about to head to Mr. K's suite when the door to the games room opens. Ms. Appleby enters carrying her clipboard and pen. The conversation stops, and I stay where I am. *Does she have a rule against tape recorders?* Without acknowledging the residents, she gives the room a once-over and jots down notes.

"Austin," Mrs. Becker says, motioning for me to move closer to her. "Is that Ms. Appleby? *Hilary* Appleby?"

When I nod, Mrs. Becker smiles. "Hilary!" she calls out.

Ms. Appleby looks our way and recognition flashes across her face. "Mrs. Becker?"

My teacher stands up and holds out her arms for a hug. I'm stunned when Ms. Appleby goes to her. *What the—?*

"I taught Hilary sixth grade!" Mrs. Becker explains to everyone.

"I can't believe you remember me," Ms. Appleby says.

Mrs. Becker gives her a warm smile. "I remember your gran too. She used to volunteer in our class. How's she doing?"

Ms. Appleby blinks, then clears her throat as if the question has caught her off-guard. "Oh, um, Gran died last year."

All the old people murmur consoling words. Mrs. Becker frowns. "I'm so sorry. That must have been hard. You two were so close."

Ms. Appleby nods, fingering her charm bracelet. "It was. I moved in with her for a while, to help out. I did the best I could but," she breaks off shaking her head. "It got to be too much." Ms. Appleby gazes around the games room wistfully. "I wish we could have afforded a place like Brayside. She'd have loved it here."

Mrs. Fradette, Mr. Singh, and Miss Lin exchange glances. I bet they're thinking the same thing as I am. *She couldn't keep her gran safe, so she's making up for it now.*

"I still can't believe you're here!" she says, brightening. "Are you visiting someone?"

Mrs. Becker points to me. "I'm Austin's teacher. He has something for Mr. Kowalski. You know, I think you might like to see what it is. Why don't you come with us to deliver it?"

Ms. Appleby hesitates. "I wish I could, but I've got a lot of work to do."

"Hilary, *this* is the work you need to do." Hearing Mrs. Becker's teacher voice outside of school makes me stand a little straighter. It has the same effect on Ms. Appleby.

Ms. Appleby stands stiffly beside Mrs. Becker when I knock on Mr. K's door. It takes him a while to answer. As soon as he sees me, he says, "I'm not up for a visit today." I don't think he even notices Mrs. Becker and Ms. Appleby.

"I know," I say quickly. "I heard about Mrs. K. I brought you something. It's for her. And you too. I was hoping you could take it to the hospital." My words come out in a rush. "Can I come in for just a minute? I want to show it to you."

Reluctantly, he agrees and shuffles aside. Mrs. Becker and Ms. Appleby stay in the hallway as I go into his suite, but the door stays open.

I find an outlet and plug in the recorder. I'm about to press Play when I glance over at Mr. K. He looks hopeless. *What if this doesn't work? Or what if it makes Mr. K feel worse? The person he loves most in the world is slipping away from him. Can a few songs really bring her back?*

I shut my eyes and push my finger down on the Play button.

"'Dancing in the Dark,'" he says right away. "Our song!

How'd you…?" He looks to his hi-fi where the record sits, and back to the tape.

"I found it on the computer and recorded it. I thought you could play it for Mrs. K when you visit her."

For a minute he doesn't say anything. He sits and listens with watery eyes. When the next song comes on, his lips curve into a sad smile.

It's "Chattanooga Choo Choo," the song he requested the first time he danced with Mrs. K. "I see what you're doing," he says to me. "But she's so weak. I was with her all morning. She didn't open her eyes once. I think she's giving up."

I ball my hands into fists and shake my head. "Mrs. K wouldn't do that."

"Austin," he says gently. And I know he's going to say something to console me, but I don't let him.

"You've gotta try," I say, my voice cracking. "Don't let her go without at least trying."

Mr. K's chin trembles. He doesn't say anything for a few minutes. I wipe away the tears on my cheeks. "You stood up for her before, you can do it again." I want these songs to work. "Play them for her, okay? And tell her I said hello, and that I miss her. We need her back here, Mr. K."

I leave the tape recorder on the table and head for the door. But then I change my mind and do something I've never done before. I lean over and give him a hug. He holds onto me for a long time, needing me as much as I need him.

I go to the hallway and shut the door after me. From Mr. K's suite, "Dancing in the Dark" plays again.

"I hope the music works," Mrs. Becker says, as Ms. Appleby and I walk her to the entrance. She's collected her coat and said good-bye to the residents in the games room.

"Me too," I say. I know it's a long shot. Mrs. K needs a miracle, not music.

Mrs. Becker wraps her scarf around her neck and turns to Ms. Appleby. "Working here must be so rewarding."

Ms. Appleby opens her mouth to say something, then closes it.

"What is it?" Mrs. Becker asks. "Hilary?"

I'm shocked to see Ms. Appleby's eyes fill with tears. "It's harder than I thought it would be," she whispers.

"What is?" Mrs. Becker's voice is soft.

"This job."

"Austin, can you give us a minute?" Mrs. Becker asks. She leads Ms. Appleby over to the couch by the fireplace. I pretend to busy myself at the reception desk, standing close enough that I can hear their conversation. I know it's rude, but I'm curious.

"The residents don't like me, and I don't know why. I'm keeping them safe. I'm doing all the things I wanted Gran's care home to do. But everyone acts like I'm...the enemy."

"Oh, I'm sure that's not true," Mrs. Becker says. "They'd like you if they got to know you."

Ms. Appleby snorts. "How am I supposed to that?" she asks, like it's the hardest thing in the world.

She really has no idea, I think to myself. That's when I start to feel bad for Ms. Appleby. She's so caught up in her role as assistant director, she doesn't know how to be herself. "You could let people call you by your first name," I blurt, forgetting I'm not supposed to be listening. "Sorry," I say catching Mrs. Becker's look of disapproval, "but it's true. None of the residents call anyone else by their last name, not even Charlie.

"I thought it would make them respect me," Ms. Appleby says sheepishly. I'm about to snort, but catch myself in time.

"What other suggestions do you have?" Mrs. Becker asks me.

"Well, since you asked, talk to them. Invite everyone to the games room for a cup of tea and a chat."

Ms. Appleby looks skeptical. "What if no one shows up?"

"They will," I say with confidence. "Trust me, old people love to talk." Especially Mrs. Gelman, I almost add, but decide to let her figure that out on her own.

Chapter 48

Maggie

Mrs. Alvarez calls a meeting for the whole cast at lunch the next day. Maggie scans the crowd for Ndidi but can't find her.

"Girls, I wanted you to hear this from me first. For personal reasons, Ndidi has decided to drop out of the musical."

There is a chorus of gasps. Maggie gets a knot in her stomach when Mrs. Alvarez's eyes fall on her. "Maggie will be taking on the role of Annie for all the performances."

A month ago, Maggie would have loved to hear those words come from her teacher's mouth, but not now.

"There's no time to waste, girls. Let's get started. If you're not in today's scenes, set design can use your help in the art room."

Maggie smiles weakly at the comments of encouragement from the other girls. The role of Annie belongs to Ndidi, not her.

Halfway through rehearsal, Maggie is allowed to take five. She's still wearing her tap shoes, the shiny ones with the ribbons. They click as she walks and the sound echoes in the empty hall. She gets out her phone and taps a text message to Ndidi.

I hope everything is okay with your mom. I'm here if you need me.

"Maggie?"

At the sight of Brianne, Maggie's guard goes up. *Is she here on Lexi's orders? Sent to rattle me and make me doubt myself?*

"I just wanted to congratulate you and see how you're doing." Brianne sounds sincere.

Maggie wants to trust her. "I'm okay. A little nervous. I wasn't expecting the news about Ndidi."

"You'll do great," Brianne says. The two girls are quiet for a moment, both lost in their thoughts. "Did you really tell Lexi to stick it in her ear?"

Maggie hesitates before nodding. Brianne's grin surprises her. "Did she do this?" Brianne does a perfect impression of Lexi's angry scowl.

Despite herself, Maggie snickers and nods.

"Lexi's not as popular as she thinks. A lot of girls don't like her. It's just that no one has the guts to stand up to her."

This surprises Maggie. Was telling a popular girl like Lexi to stick it in her ear gutsy—or foolish?

"I wanted to try out for a role, but Lexi said it would suck if I got a better part than she did. So, I didn't." Brianne sighs. "My mom was mad. 'All those years of dance lessons, for what?'" Brianne imitates her mom. Now that Maggie thinks about it, casting Brianne as a chorus member is a waste of her talent.

"We'll need a new understudy if I'm going to be Annie for all the performances," Maggie says. "You should talk to Mrs. Alvarez."

Brianne's eyebrows go up. "You think I'm good enough?"

"Yeah," Maggie says. "Of course, you are. And if you do get the part, then *you* can tell Lexi to stick it in her ear."

Chapter 49

Austin

I pause to stamp the snow off my boots before I go into Brayside. I sigh when I see a new sign outside. It says, Caution: Sidewalk May Be Icy. I guess Ms. Appleby didn't listen to Mrs. Becker's advice after all.

The sign isn't what's really bothering me though. All day I've been wondering about Mrs. K.

When I get inside, I'm surprised to see the Valentine's decorations are back up. In fact, there's more than before. Isaac's packing up his tool kit at the reception desk, and waves at me.

"Why are those back up?" I ask, pointing to the sparkly cupid hanging in the window.

"Ms. Appleby had a change of *heart*," he says, and grins.

I groan. "I thought Grandpa had the worst jokes."

Isaac laughs. "Guess what else happened?" He reaches into the back pocket of his coveralls and pulls out an envelope.

"Is that—?"

"Yeah, all the money for my niece's gift!"

"Where was it?"

"Charlie had it."

"Charlie!?"

"He didn't take it on purpose. He scooped it out of the drawer with some other files. Didn't even know he had it until this morning."

I think back to the Sunday I saw Charlie leaving. It never occurred to me that he would have a key to that drawer, or that he'd have taken anything from it. My eyes search for the surveillance camera over the nurses' station, but it's gone.

"Ms. Appleby decided we didn't need it after all," Isaac says following my gaze. "I think things might be loosening up a little."

"Really?"

Isaac nods. "She had tea with Mrs. O'Brien this afternoon and helped Mr. Santos with his crossword puzzle." I frown because solving the clues for Mr. Santos is my job. Then again, if it means Ms. Appleby is getting to know the residents, I guess that's a good thing.

"Great news about the money," I say when I see Mary Rose at the nurses' station. I thought she'd be happy too, but her face is serious.

"You need to go see Mr. Kowalski. He has something to tell you."

My breath gets lodged in my throat. "Is it—" I can't bring myself to say the words out loud, but I really hope Mrs. K is all right. Mary Rose's face doesn't give anything away. She's been here a long time and has seen a lot of residents come and go. She's good at holding in her emotions.

"He's waiting for you," she says, opening a patient's file.

"Is it—?" I start again, but Mary Rose waves her hand at me.

Part of me wants to run to his suite, and the other part wants to crawl. When I get to his door, I raise my hand to knock and say a quick prayer that Mrs. K made it through the night.

Mr. K opens the door, his eyes are red and he's got a balled-up tissue in his hand. I stand there, afraid to step into the room. Residents, people I've cared about, have passed away before, and it's hard. *Really* hard. "Austin," he says. His voice breaks, and I can't tell if he wanted to say something more, or if that was it, just my name.

"You better come in," he says and wipes his eyes. The tape player from school is on the coffee table. *Did he get to play the songs for Mrs. K? Or…was it too late?* I shuffle to the couch and wish Harvey, or Bertie, was with me so I'd have something comforting if there's bad news coming.

"I called my daughter last night and asked her to take me to the hospital. I'd been listening to those songs and I thought, *If Alice is going to go, I want it to be with me beside her, and these songs in her head.*" Mr. K breaks off and takes a minute to collect himself. "I plugged the recorder in and pressed Play. Then I pulled the chair up close to her bed and held her hand. I started humming along with the music, then kind of, you know, swaying. I thought, *What the heck? This is Alice's moment,* so I lifted her hand and started dipping it up and down with the music, as if we were dancing.

"If someone had come in, they'd have thought I was bonkers. We went through the tape once, and then I pressed Rewind and played it again. It was like Alice and I were in our own little world. I started talking about the first time we danced together in Neepawa. And that was when I felt it." Mr. K looks at me. "She squeezed my hand. At first, I thought I'd imagined it. I told her to come back to me. I said, 'Our dance isn't over yet.'" Mr. K pauses. "Then her eyelids fluttered."

He wipes his eyes and looks at me. I'm holding my breath waiting to hear his next words. "She's awake Austin. She's weak and she can't talk much, but she woke up."

I stare at Mr. K, not trusting myself to talk. Now I see those aren't tears of sadness on Mr. K's face. They're tears of joy.

Chapter 50

Maggie

"We're going to work on Hannigan and Rooster's scene for the rest of rehearsal," Mrs. Alvarez says. She rubs her forehead, as if she has headache. She probably does. "Everyone who isn't in it can leave."

Maggie looks up with a start. That means she has almost an hour until her dad is going to pick her up on his way home from work. The text she sent to Ndidi a while ago has gone unanswered. Despite their promise not to let other people get between them, Maggie hopes Ndidi doesn't think she's happy about being Annie. She'd gladly hand it back if it meant Ndidi's mom was okay.

A few of the girls decide to go to Tubby's. "Want to come with us?" Brianne asks.

Maggie is torn. She's already texted her dad to ask him to pick her up at Brayside. With an hour to wait, she can check in on everyone.

"Lexi won't be there," Brianne adds.

"It's not that," Maggie says and gives a hurried explanation about Ms. Appleby, the dance, and Mrs. Kowalski.

Brianne's eyes widen. "Wow. A lot goes on over there. I thought it was just a bunch of old people."

Maggie bites back a laugh. If things weren't so tense at Brayside, she'd invite Brianne to come with her. Ndidi had a good time, maybe Brianne would too. In fact—Maggie looks at the girls left in the theater —maybe they all would.

"Maggie! What are you doing here? You poor girl, you look half frozen. Did you walk all the way from school?" Mary Rose asks from the nurses' desk.

It really isn't that far, but the tights she wears do nothing to stop the cold, and her legs are numb. "Yes," she shivers.

"Go stand by the fire," Mary Rose suggests. Maggie does a double take at the crackling fire. The sign posted by Ms. Appleby banning them is gone. And the Valentine's decorations are back up.

Mary Rose catches her looking around the foyer and says, "*Hilary* and I had a long talk this morning."

Maggie's eyebrows shoot up. "And?" Is Mary Rose is going to announce she's leaving? If she goes, the rest of the staff might follow.

Maggie sighs with relief when Mary Rose grins. "I think she's starting to understand what running a place like Brayside is all about." With Mary Rose staying, Maggie can only hope Mrs. Fradette will too.

"And we've had more good news. Mrs. Kowalski woke up! They're hoping to move her out of the ICU tomorrow, and if she keeps improving, she'll be back at Brayside soon. Austin's with Mr. Kowalski in his suite, but the others are in the games room."

Maggie makes her way there, rubbing her hands together to bring feeling back into her fingers. When she steps inside, she sees almost all the residents, and Ms. Appleby, who has the dreaded clipboard on her lap.

Mrs. Fradette gestures for Maggie to join them. As she passes Ms. Appleby, she glances at what Ms. Appleby is writing. It's a list titled Resident Suggestions.

"As for the dance, it's not that I'm against having fun," Ms. Appleby says. That gets an eyeroll from Mrs. Fradette. "But what about the residents who don't have a partner? Or who are like Mr. Kowalski? A Valentine's dance could be triggering for him with his wife in the hospital."

"You're trying to protect us," Mrs. Fradette says. "But that's not what we need."

Ms. Appleby looks confused. "My job is to protect you."

"We aren't children." Mrs. O'Brien's voice is firm, but kind.

Maggie could add a lot to this discussion. She's seen how the residents care for each other, for the people who work at Brayside, and even for her and Austin.

"We're a family," Mrs. Fradette adds. "Looking out for each other is what we do."

"We knew the dance would be hard for Bob. That's why we elected him Duke of the Valentine's Dance," Mr. Singh tells her.

"We've all lived long lives," Mrs. Fradette says. She gives a barky laugh. "Some longer than others! And trust me, we've had obstacles. We want to finish our days in comfort in a place that feels like a home. Not a prison."

Ms. Appleby winces. "Brayside feels like a jail?"

"Yes, dear," Mrs. O'Brien says, but she's smiling. "We know you care, but all the rules!" she shakes her head. "They're going to drive us away, not keep us safe."

"What about Harvey?" Maggie asks. "Do I still need to get permission when he visits?"

Ms. Appleby glances at the residents. They all shake their heads. "He is a comfort dog," Miss Lin says. "Whether he's certified or not."

Ms. Appleby's mouth twitches. "I'd still like notice when

you're bringing him, but he can roam freely when he's here. Not in the dining room, of course."

"No," Maggie says, shaking her head and holding back a smile. "Not in the dining room."

Ms. Appleby gets up to leave. "I better notify the staff of the changes. I was also thinking…the library doesn't get used much." There's a collective gasp of worry. *What's she thinking?* "Maybe I could lead a writing group. I'm sure lots of you have great stories to tell." Her hand goes to the charm bracelet on her wrist. "I know my gran did."

Maggie shares a smile with Mrs. Fradette. She knows for certain that's the truth.

Chapter 51

Harvey

Harvey has been waiting all day for Maggie. It's a joyful moment when he hears the garage door open.

"Hi, Harvey," Maggie says and bends down so he can lick her nose. She's been at Brayside. Familiar smells linger on her. He senses something else too—a heaviness. What has happened to make her sigh the way she does when she flops onto her bed? Harvey jumps up and splays his legs behind him, like an otter. Maggie runs her hand down his head, and back to his tail. When her phone rings, Maggie jumps for it. "Hi, Ndidi." She sounds relieved. "How are you?"

Harvey's sharp ears pick up the voice on the other end.

"I'm okay. I got your text. My mom's home. I wanted to let you know."

"How is she?"

Ndidi doesn't say anything for a minute. "The doctors switched the chemo drugs. The other ones were making her too sick. My auntie is coming to stay with us for a few weeks. She'll be around to look after Koby."

"That's good, right? Now you'll have some help. You can," there's a small catch to Maggie's voice that she tries to hide, "come back to the musical."

Ndidi sucks in a breath. "That's why I wanted to talk to you. Mrs. Alvarez…"

But Maggie doesn't let Ndidi finish. She goes back to rubbing Harvey's back, twisting bits of his fur between her fingers. "Honestly, it's fine. It's your role, Ndidi." Maggie is calm when she says this, but Harvey senses sadness too. Maggie isn't the happy-go-lucky girl he first met four years ago who skipped and giggled. But Harvey isn't the same puppy he was either. They've both grown up.

"Can you do one favor for me?" Maggie asks. "It's a secret, for now, anyway."

As Maggie explains her plan to Ndidi, Harvey drifts off. He hears his name once or twice, but doesn't stir. Lying beside his Maggie is where he wants to be.

Chapter 52

Austin

"Amar, I have something to tell you…"
"Amar, I know this sucks…"
"About Edu-Trek…"

I've run through so many versions of how to tell Amar I'm not going on Edu-Trek that when he comes into homeroom, my mind goes blank. I can't remember what one I settled on.

"You've got your form, right?" he asks because today is the deadline.

I fidget with a pen, avoiding looking at Amar. Mom got the job—the one she interviewed for. She's excited because it's more money, better hours, and close to home. It's a win-win-win. But she doesn't start for two weeks, which means I still don't have the deposit for Edu-Trek.

"Right?" Amar asks again.

I take a deep breath. "There's something I need to tell you."

Mrs. Becker holds up her hands to quiet everyone down. She looks directly at me and my open mouth. "Tell you later," I say to Amar.

"Leave your books at your desk. We're going to the gym for an assembly." There's lots of groaning because the assemblies are boring and sitting on the hard gym floor makes our butts numb. "Would you prefer a math quiz?" Mrs. Becker asks sarcastically. Everyone stops complaining.

"What's the assembly for?" Amar asks.

"I mentioned it at the beginning of the week," Mrs. Becker tells him. I tune her out because my mind is still on Edu-Trek. If only Mom had got the job a month ago, things might be different.

Our class is the last to arrive at the gym. We sit down at the back. Ms. Khokhar stands with a microphone at the front. She looks extra dressed up today. A man who looks kind of familiar is sitting behind her. I tilt my head, trying to place him.

When everyone is settled, Ms. Khokhar starts off talking about kindness and how Valentine's Day, which is just around the corner, is a day to acknowledge the people we care about. "You have no doubt noticed that we have a guest here today. I'd like to introduce Mr. Reggie Diggs."

My mouth drops open. *Reggie Diggs? The baseball player?*

"Dude! I knew that was him!" Amar elbows me.

The gym erupts into applause as Reggie steps up to the microphone.

"The Digger!" Amar shouts out and cheers.

Reggie laughs. "That's right, that was my nickname. I used to play ball, but now I run an organization called Homerun Heroes. We're committed to sharing stories about young people making a difference. I go coast to coast to meet them and let them know that what they're doing matters. Your principal, Ms. Khokhar, reached out to me last week and shared a story about someone here. When I heard it, I knew this was a kid I had to meet!"

He pulls a paper out of his jacket pocket and unfolds it. "Here's what Ms. Khokhar wrote to me.

Dear Mr. Diggs,
I'm the principal at Oscar Peterson Middle School.
I've recently learned how one of our students helps
the community."

I wish Grandpa was here, I think as Reggie keeps talking, *because he's never gonna believe the Digger was at our school!* But then, I hear my name and I look up. Everyone's eyes, including Amar's, Ms. Khokhar's, and Mrs. Becker's, are turned in my direction.

"Austin is in seventh grade and goes to Brayside Retirement Villa almost every day after school. According to the nursing staff and the assistant director, he has a special relationship with many of the residents, but it's what he's done for the Kowalskis that I want to share with you.

Bob Kowalski and his wife have been married for over sixty years and live at Brayside. Recently, Mrs. Kowalski was admitted to the hospital due to pneumonia. As her condition declined, Austin's concern for Mr. Kowalski grew. He took it upon himself to visit more often to cheer him up. After hearing stories about how the couple met, he made up a playlist of songs special to the Kowalskis, recorded them, and gave them to Mr. Kowalski to play for her.

To everyone's surprise—and joy—Mrs. Kowalski improved. In fact, she's expected to make a full recovery and join her husband back at Brayside. To Mr. Kowalski, and the other residents, Austin is a hero. He shows compassion and always acts with kindness. He even rescued a puppy from an alley earlier this year. I can't think of a better Homerun Hero than Austin."

Mr. Diggs puts down the letter. Now, *everyone* is looking at me, so I stare straight ahead.

"Austin, you are a true Homerun Hero. It's an honor to give you this award. Please, come up to the front."

Everyone is clapping. I'm still shocked that Reggie Diggs is in my school, never mind that he's giving me an award! It's kind of a blur about how I get up there, but all of a sudden, Ms. Khokhar is shaking my hand, and then I'm face-to-face with Reggie Diggs. A professional photographer snaps photos with a fancy camera.

"Thank you for making a difference," Reggie says. He hands me a plaque. It's got Homerun Hero and my name engraved on it.

"How about a few words, Austin?" Reggie points to the microphone.

Speaking in front of everyone is the last thing I want to do, but I can't say no to Reggie Diggs!

I take a step toward the microphone. Reggie lowers it for me because he's so much taller. I look out at the crowd and that's when I see Mom and Grandpa standing at the back.

Mrs. Fradette is there too, beside Mr. Singh. Mrs. O'Brien and Miss Lin are next, and then Mary Rose and Louise. Mr. Santos, Mrs. Gelman and even Mrs. Gustafson is in her wheelchair, pushed by Ms. Appleby.

But it's when I see Mr. Kowalski that a lump forms in my throat. He's wiping tears from his eyes.

Somewhere, I think, *Mr. Pickering might be watching this too.*

I'm so stunned to see all of them, my mind goes blank. "Wow," I start. My voice sounds weird amplified. "I never expected this. I'm not even sure I deserve it, honestly." I swallow. My mouth is dry and my hands are shaking. "Brayside is kind of like home, and the residents and staff there have become family. And you'd do anything for your family, right?" I look at Mom. She's not doing a very good job of holding back her tears. Grandpa's got his arm around her. "Thanks so much, Mr. Diggs for coming to our school. My grandpa's right there and he's a big fan." I point him out and Grandpa waves. "So's my friend, Amar." There's laughter as Amar gives Reggie a standing ovation. "Thank you also to Ms. Khokhar and Mrs. Becker for organizing all this. It's…well, I never expected it." I get a little choked up then and stand back.

Reggie reaches into his pocket and pulls out an envelope. "As well as the plaque, there's also a cash award," he says. "A cheque for a thousand dollars."

I almost drop the plaque. I stare at Reggie. He nods at me to take it. "Go on, son. You've earned it."

My fingers tremble as I take the envelope from him. I've never had this much money in my life. My first thought is *I better not lose this.*

My second thought is *Edu-Trek.*

"I can't believe I met the Digger," Grandpa says later that night. He's staring at the signed baseball in his hands and sounds like he's twelve years old again. Bertie's lying in my lap. I run my hands over her velvety ears.

The Homerun Hero plaque is propped up on the coffee table. Mom keeps glancing at it, a proud smile on her face.

The rest of the day at school was a whirlwind of congratulations and high-fives. I never got around to telling Amar about Edu-Trek. Even though I'm a thousand dollars richer, it's still not enough to pay for the whole trip.

After going to the vet, a little piece of me wonders if I should save the money in case Bertie needs it. Or the car breaks down again. But most of me wants to plunk the cash down on Mrs. Becker's desk and say, "Sign me up!" and worry about the last couple hundred plus spending money later.

I fall asleep that night hoping that by the morning I'll know what I should do.

Chapter 53

Maggie

A burst of warm air hits Maggie when the front doors at Brayside slide open. Harvey takes the lead and bolts inside. He's got a bright red Valentine's Day bandana knotted at his neck and looks very smart. Maggie, Ndidi, and ten members of the cast, including Lexi and Brianne, follow behind. Mrs. Alvarez is there too. And so is Sooyeon.

"What's this?" Mr. Singh asks, taking in the crowd of girls. His scooter is decorated with red tinsel, and there's a heart on the basket. He's dressed for the occasion too, wearing a red vest and a bow tie. Are you all here for the dance?"

"Not exactly," Maggie says.

Mrs. Alvarez's eyes land on the grand piano sitting in front of the dining room.

As the girls and Mrs. Alvarez get settled, the residents trickle into the foyer and are directed to their seats by Ms. Appleby...um...*Hilary*. It had taken some convincing, and a detailed plan, but Maggie had been overjoyed when she finally agreed to let the cast sing for the residents.

Maggie is chatting with Mrs. Fradette and doesn't notice the man at the door until Louise groans. "Oh, no. It's that health and safety officer. Of all days for him to show up!"

Maggie turns to the door to see Mr. Chang. He's eyeing up the foyer like it's a new germ specimen. "Are we breaking any rules?" Maggie asks.

"I don't think so, but he's a real stickler. The last thing we need is for Hilary to have second thoughts about loosening up the rules."

Mr. Chang scans the room and frowns. "What's going on here?"

"A concert for the residents," Hilary says, "to celebrate Valentine's Day." The confidence ebbs from her voice. Maggie glances at the residents as Harvey wanders between them, enjoying the attention.

"Is that a dog?" Mr. Chang asks.

"Yes, but he's hypo-allergenic!" Hilary says quickly. "And very well-behaved. That's his owner, Maggie."

Maggie gives Mr. Chang a nervous wave. "You're the girl

I met last time," he says. "This is your dog?"

Maggie nods slowly. "His name is Harvey."

Mr. Chang crouches down. "Here, Harvey," he calls. Maggie imagines Mr. Chang picking Harvey up by the scruff of his neck and tossing him out the front doors. She opens her mouth to tell him to leave Harvey alone when Mr. Chang looks up at her. "Westies are my favorite breed. I had one when I was a kid. His name was Angus."

The words Maggie was about to say stall in her throat. "Westies are the best," she says. Harvey takes that as his cue to trot over to Mr. Chang and say hello. His tail wags as he puts his front paws on the man's knees and licks his nose. Mr. Chang laughs out loud and pats Harvey on the head.

"That's our Harvey," Mrs. Fradette says. "What a charmer!"

"And our number one mouse catcher!" says Mr. Singh loudly, which gets him shushed by everyone.

Thankfully, Mr. Chang is oblivious. He's too caught up with Harvey. Maggie doesn't know why she's surprised. If anyone can melt someone's heart, it's her Harvey.

When the show is about to begin, Maggie looks out at the audience. Mrs. O'Brien and Miss Lin are in the front row. Behind them, Sooyeon has found a place between Mr. Singh and Mrs. Fradette. Mrs. Fradette's Valentine's Day outfit breaks all the fashion rules. Reds, pinks, and purples clash, and huge heart earrings dangle to her shoulders.

From down the hall, there's some fanfare. Austin and Artie hold their hands to their mouths as if they're blowing trumpets. "*Badadadum.*" Then Mr. Kowalski's door opens. He's wearing his Duke of Valentine's Day sash and a crown. He gives a royal wave to the gathered crowd, clearly enjoying the attention.

"Oh my gosh, that's hilarious," Ndidi whispers to Maggie. Sooyeon stands up to take some photos for Mrs. Kowalski.

When he's seated, Mr. Kowalski commands, "Let the festivities begin!" in a booming voice. First up is "It's The Hard Knock Life." All the girls sing and the residents thoroughly enjoy themselves. There's an enthusiastic round of applause when they finish.

"If you liked that, you'll love our next song," Ndidi says. She smiles at the audience and her eyes fall on Mrs. Fradette. "'Sandy' sung by Maggie, with special guest Harvey!" Ndidi steps back and beams at Maggie as she takes center stage, dragging a chair with her.

This is Maggie's chance to perform a solo in front of an audience, and she intends to make the most of it.

"Here, Sandy," Maggie calls, and just like they practiced last night, Harvey jumps up and turns to the audience. The song is about having a dog who somehow knows just what his person needs. As she finishes belting out "Sandy," Mrs. Fradette gets to her feet for a standing ovation. Not all the residents can jump up as quickly as she can, so Maggie takes it as a compliment when a few others try.

Maggie bows and Harvey jumps down to congratulate her too. Singing at Brayside might not be the same as an audience of hundreds in a real theater, but Maggie isn't complaining. She sang in front of people who mattered to her and can see the pride on their faces.

"For our final number, Ndidi Udo will perform 'Tomorrow,'" Maggie says, and then steps back. At Maggie's suggestion, Ndidi will sing unaccompanied, just as she did in the theater. Chills run up Maggie's spine as soon as Ndidi sings the first few notes. The other girls feel it too. Many of them haven't heard Ndidi sing this way—her voice is full of heartbreak but also hope.

It is the perfect song to share with the residents, and when Ndidi is done, there's not a dry eye in the house.

Chapter 54

Harvey

The dance is in full swing, but the music in the games room is too loud for Harvey. He retreats to the foyer and hops up on the couch. Normally this isn't allowed, and he'd be ordered to get down, but no one else is around right now. Maggie and Austin are inside getting a lesson in the waltz from Mr. Kowalski.

Harvey lies down His chin hangs over the edge a little.

The games room door opens and Ms. Appleby comes out. She walks toward the reception desk and pauses when she sees Harvey. "Look at you," she says. Harvey raises one eyebrow and keeps his eyes straight ahead. Maybe if he doesn't look at her, she won't notice him. She comes to the couch and stands over him with her hands on her hips. Harvey waits to be ordered off.

But the order doesn't come.

Instead, Ms. Appleby sits down. Harvey's spine stiffens at her nearness. He's still not sure about this person and can tell she feels the same about him.

Ms. Appleby opens her palm in front of Harvey's nose. Her bracelet jingles in a pleasing way. He gives her hand a perfunctory sniff. Tentatively, she reaches out and pats him on the back. Harvey stays still. Next comes a gentle scratch behind the ears. By scent, he knows this woman, but something about her has changed. To test his theory, Harvey rolls to his side, inviting her to give him a belly rub.

Ms. Appleby laughs softly and complies. "You know, you're actually very cute," she whispers. "But don't tell anyone I said that. I have an image to uphold." Harvey licks her hand in appreciation.

The secret is safe with him.

Chapter 55

Austin

Watching old people dance is more entertaining than I thought it would be. First of all, some of them, like Mrs. Fradette, can really move. No surprise there. She's been on the floor the whole time. She's got this "jazz hands" move that she's showing to Maggie, Sooyeon, and Ndidi. Mr. Singh spent the first half hour demonstrating the pivot action on the Cobra GT4—also impressive. Mr. Santos's dancing isn't very graceful. He's so lanky that when he moves his arms, he flaps like a flightless bird. That doesn't stop Miss Lin from trying to keep up with him though.

But it's Mr. Kowalski who's having the best time. I have

ten minutes of video to show Mrs. K. All the ladies want a turn dancing with him. I made sure to take "Dancing in the Dark" off the playlist. I'll save that one for when Mrs. K is back at Brayside.

Maggie steps off the dance floor to stand beside me. "You're a really good singer," I tell her over the music.

She shrugs off my compliment.

"No, really. I wish I was gifted at something like that. Had a talent, or was good at school, or sports. I'm just," I shrug, "you know. Average."

Maggie glares at me. "Austin! You got an award for being awesome—that's not," she imitates my shrug, "*average.*" She gives my arm a good-natured punch. One thing about Maggie is that she's become a lot more confident this year. A little sassier too.

Mr. Kowalski comes sailing by with Mrs. O'Brien. "I can't wait to take Alice dancing!" he says to me. "I forgot how much fun this was!"

The Valentine's Day dance is a huge success. When it's almost over, Ms. Appleby opens the games room door to come inside, but she's not the first one through. That honor goes to Harvey who, once again, is in the lead.

"Harvey," I call. "Come here." I crouch down as he runs across the room. With his mouth open, I could swear he's grinning at me.

There's a *toot* behind me. I turn to find Mr. Singh.

"The social committee wanted to give you something for organizing the music," Mr. Singh says, handing me an envelope.

"You didn't have to do that," I say.

"We didn't have to. We wanted to," Mr. Singh says firmly. I look inside the envelope. It's a check from the Brayside Social Committee, and it's for three hundred dollars!

My heart jumps. "Mr. Singh, I can't take it," I say and pass it back to him.

"Nonsense! Look around!"

I do. All the residents are enjoying themselves. Even Hilary's having fun. She got pulled into Mrs. Fradette's jazz hands tutorial.

"None of this would have happened without you."

There's no point trying to argue with him. "Thank you, Mr. Singh." Three hundred dollars means I have enough for Edu-Trek, and even a little spending money. As soon as I get home, I'll send Mrs. Becker an e-mail. And then I'll text Amar to let him know we can be roomies after all.

Maggie and her friends invited me to join them at a restaurant called Tubby's after the dance, but I said no. I need to send that e-mail to Mrs. Becker. There's new snow falling and under the glow of the streetlights the flakes sparkle like diamonds. Everyone enjoyed the Valentine's celebration. The best part, though, was hearing Maggie sing. I get a little twinge in my chest thinking about it.

Somewhere up ahead there's a familiar *yip*. "Bertie?" I call out. Sure enough, Mom's on the other end of the leash getting dragged on the snowy sidewalk by my puppy. As soon as Bertie knows for sure it's me, she goes into overdrive, ears flopping all over the place as she races in my direction.

I crouch down. With only a few feet left, Mom lets go of the leash and Bertie races into my arms. Right where she belongs.

Acknowledgments

Since I never get tired of thanking the crew at Pajama Press, I'll start by acknowledging the heart and soul they put into each book they publish. Thank you to Gail Winskill for unflagging leadership, support, and wonderful chats. To Kathryn Cole, who made the book better in all kinds of ways and deserves a crown of gold stars. Thank you to Erin Alladin, Dagmawit Dejene, and Lorena González Guillén. You really are a dream team.

The adorable illustrations that start each chapter are thanks to Tara Anderson. Her art brings so much life to the pages. Thank you, Tara!

Thank you to Dr. Marta Gunn of the Alberta Animal Rescue Crew Society Veterinary Hospital for answering my questions. You'll notice the real Dr. Gunn's name is used in the book. There are a few other people whose names I've borrowed. Rabia Khokhar and Miriam Becker are two dedicated teachers who inspired the characters in the book. I've known so many amazing educators, I'll have to keep writing to get all their names in print!

As with the other Harvey Stories, my uncle Wayne Pickering helped guide the historical sections of this book. I'm so grateful for his never-ending expertise and incredible memory. Any errors are my fault, not his!

Sometimes, as an author, you get the opportunity to connect with groups of students. It was such fun to visit (virtually) Mr. Bannerman's Grade 5 class of 2021 from Central School, Swift Current a few times. Thanks to their wonderful Teacher-Librarian Lori Kruk for starting the ball rolling—one more way TLs are amazing!

Spreading the word about a new book can be tricky. I'm so grateful to Kathie MacIsaac, Laurie Hnatiuk, Helen Kubiw, Julie DenOuden, Alexis Ennis, Tiffany Loveland, the folks at #BookPosse, and of course, the good people at McNally Robinson, my beloved indie bookstore, for all the book love.